TRACK FOUR IS NOT ABOUT YOU

Contents

Content Note

There is a brief moment of misgendering in this story. It's treated as a mistake and acknowledged by the narrator before the scene moves on.

Preface

*Cam, Romi, and Skye's story continues in **Kissing The Opps**.*

Dedication

This book did not arrive easily. We beefed back and forth before we said "okay, fine, let's do this."

Thank you to these people who help talk me back from the ledge, or are just awesome people in general:

A.J.B.S., Brianna Mbog, Terri Ronald, Frankie Fyre, Cheril N. Clarke, Mary C.,

Tuesday Harper, Felene Cayetano, Naomi Rivers, Evie Marque, Kellie W.,

Tonja K. Johnson, Adrian J. Smith, Tessa Stone, Joy W., Lici, Chelle,

Ava Freeman, Christa Hickcox, Bryce Oakley, Ruby Landers, Cheyenne Browning

Rest in Power, Glenda J. Johnson and Harper Glenn

Playlist

Thinkin Bout You — Frank Ocean

Don't Wish Me Well — Solange

Bitch, Don't Kill My Vibe — Kendrick Lamar

4:44 — JAY-Z

Cold — Maxwell

6 Inch [feat. The Weeknd] — Beyoncé

Immigrant Song – Remaster — Led Zeppelin

See You Again [feat. Kali Uchis] — Tyler, The Creator

Happiness Over Everything (H.O.E.) [feat. Miguel and Future] -Jhené
Aiko

Sooner or Later – N.E.R.D
The Math – Jill Scott
Redbone — Childish Gambino

Folded — Kehlani

Is It Mine [feat. Lady London] — Coco Jones

A Day In The Life – Remastered 2009 — The Beatles

Reason To Stay — Olivia Dean

Weird Fishes / Arpeggi — Radiohead

Distance — Yebba

Come Home [feat. André 3000] – Anderson .Paak

YUKON — Justin Bieber

Where This Flower Blooms [feat. Frank Ocean] — Tyler, The Creator

Good Together — Shay Lia

You can find the Spotify soundtrack below:

3 A.M. And The Mix Still Isn't Right

Shiloh

I ALWAYS WORKED BEST after midnight, after the city's white noise finally gave up. Out here in the studio, every room was padded, dead as a crypt. I liked it that way. No echoes. No sound but the machinery and my brain working overtime.

I didn't build this place out of nostalgia.

Floating floors. Every inch isolated, every soft panel tuned for absorption. Concrete gray. I rolled my cables military-tight, wiped every pedal down with isopropyl and a cloth. The air always smelled faintly of lavender oil from my diffuser (my own ratio, because store-bought was for quitters, and I could always tell when the blend was off). Vinyl wall. Dark grid, perfectly sleeved, sorted first by emotional valence, then by year. Nothing else cluttered.

Tonight, I was wrapping up Cam Wolfe's single. "Wrapping up" was a joke. I'd finished a week ago, but Cam was a perfectionist in her own way. She'd talk like she didn't care, then send a hundred tweaks at 3 a.m. on the eve of master delivery. This new tape was pure ego: sub-bass rumbling like a semi, hi-hats up top like they were trying to break glass, synths jerking in and out of key to see if I'd smooth them down. I liked a challenge. Even when her voice was engineered to start a fight in your car.

Right now, Cam was feeding herself to the monitors. I'd looped her verse, chasing the perfect midrange compression on her consonants. The chorus detonated every time:

"Queen with no subjects/just subjects to change/built your whole throne on keeping subjects in chains—"

That last word, "chains," she spat it so hard you could practically taste the enamel. I slowed the attack by a millisecond, and the difference was instant: the edges flared, sharp as a threat.

Let it loop. My left hand stalled over the board, right on my mug. The coffee was cold, but I kept sipping out of habit. Clock said 2:39 a.m. I made a note to check the mix during the day instead of these vampire hours. Not that it mattered. I already knew it would hold. Still, I triple-checked the levels. Left monitor, right, then headphones for a final pass. Spot on.

The only other light came from the main display: stems in a pale grid, little rectangles stacking up for vocals and beats, all marching in line. After a few hours, the DAW started looking like a spreadsheet from hell. Cam's voice cut through, clean as a knife:

"Queenpin, is you really the blueprint—"

I snorted. The sound hung in the dead air. That line was aimed straight at Romi Dulce. Everybody in the business would know it, even if Cam never said Romi's name. Classic: plausible deniability, enough poison in the pen to keep the blogs busy for a week.

The speakers hissed as the track played. My neck was locked up from hours in the chair, so I did a slow stretch, vertebrae popping like bubble wrap. Rolled my shoulders. In the glassy night, the only motion came from the meters twitching along with Cam's voice, like they were agreeing with her.

"I move like the sun/don't need you to cheer/still risin' each day, whether you clap or sneer."

Scrolled to the end of the session, double-clicked the final bounce. Labeled it:

CAM WOLFE—NOCTURNAL V2.

Attached the PDF for liner notes. Checked the timestamp a beat longer than I needed.

Didn't want to close the file. Not that I loved Cam's music so much—even though it scratched that itch for kinetic violence—but this was the last thing on my list before I had to face the other job. The one I'd ignored all day, and most of the night. I paused on the *X* in the corner, but my hand dropped.

Silence.

It's always a shock, the amount of dead air a just-finished track leaves. I stood up, cracked my knuckles, and took a lap around the control room. The only thing moving was the digital clock, ticking off seconds I wasn't spending working on the thing I was supposed to be doing.

My father used to joke that I inherited his work ethic but none of his coordination. "You got the genes for greatness," he'd said, "just pointed them at the wrong sport." He'd wanted a baller ready for the pro leagues, just like him. Wasted money sending me to the court I met Bishop at. Got a music nerd who met another music nerd instead. But he understood obsession, though. The kind that kept you up at 2 a.m. perfecting your craft. That part, I got from him.

I circled back to the mixing console. My phone was face-down on the edge, yellow badge glowing under the glass. Sixteen unread notifications. One from Chelsea Lam, whoever that was, stamped "urgent," the subject line screaming in all caps. I'd seen it twelve hours ago and promised myself I'd answer it tomorrow. But it pressed down on me now, thick and heavy, like an over-compressed kick drum. The rest were noise: Cam tagging me in a meme, my mastering engineer with a dumb Pixo, a bunch of group texts that only existed because their founder had zero social awareness.

I picked up the phone. My thumb didn't move. The weight of it always got me—a heavy, overbuilt slab of metal and glass, too expensive for how often I wanted to throw it off a bridge. I unlocked it, scrolled to the top.

CHELSEA LAM, Peachtree.

Subject: CONFIDENTIAL: Production Emergency—Need Your Input ASAP

She'd written it in that perfect faux-casual that only PR people can pull off:

Hey shi.ctrl, not sure what your current bandwidth is, but we've got a situation. Project isn't coming together and we need a new direction, fast. I know you two have... let's say, "collaborative chemistry." You're the only one who gets her sound. If anyone can rescue this, it's you. Think of it as a creative challenge. Please listen to the attached and let us know if you're available.

I glanced at the recipient's list, and there it was in blue hyperlink: Evienne Baptiste. Her real name, not the stage name. I hadn't seen it written out in years. It twisted something low in my gut. I locked the phone without reading further.

The blogs said a frustrated Bishop pushed until her last producer quit. Not that I had read that, or anything. Just repeating what they said.

They also said she'd gotten too big, too fast. That success had gone to her head, and she couldn't handle being part of a team anymore. That she'd outgrown everyone who'd helped her get there.

I wanted to believe that version. It was easier than the alternative that told me I'd done something wrong. Said the wrong thing. Been too controlling in the studio, too cold outside of it. Pushed too hard or not hard enough. The not knowing was worse than any explanation the blogs could offer. At least if she'd gotten too famous to care, it wasn't personal.

But late at night, when I couldn't sleep, I replayed our last sessions together. Searched for the moment I'd pushed her too hard. The moment that made her decide I wasn't worth a phone call, a text, even a goodbye fuck.

Walked to the kitchenette. Poured more coffee into the mug (it was ice-cold, bitter as fuck). Came back, sat down, forced my thumb to hold still while I opened the message.

I didn't hate Bishop. Actually, I sort of respected her for going supernova without me and never picking up the pieces. But the last time we'd spoken, I was still dumb enough to believe creative partnerships were immune to emotional blackmail. I'd spent too long engineering the mess out of my life.

I skimmed the rest of Chelsea's email. The label had already let Bishop experiment. They hired the hottest names, gave her the space to reinvent our sound. But every time, the result was the same: chaos without shape, fire without fuel. Now, they wanted a miracle. They wanted me to "take chaos and make it sound intentional." Like intention was a seasoning packet I could shake over someone else's train wreck. At the bottom, a Dropbox link to a "private, unmastered track—strictly for your ears only." Postscript: "You're the only one she'll listen to, if she'll listen at all."

They weren't forcing Bishop into a box. They were recruiting me to coax her sound into the shape it was always meant to take—because, apparently, they thought I was the only one who ever could. This, after saying no to me the first time.

Set the phone down again.

Back to the monitors. The waveform on the screen was flat as a corpse. I played a reference track from my archive, something cool and clean, no drama. I'd engineered it years back; got me my first real notice. I set it low, just enough to keep the silence from swallowing me.

But the silence kept stretching. I tapped my pen on the desk, old nervous habit from grad school. Checked the time: 3:07 a.m. My body was clocking all the tells: jaw tight, breath shallow, fingers tapping out beats against my thigh.

Sipped coffee. Stared at the phone, that yellow badge still glowing.

I looked at Chelsea's email again. The font was standard email blue, but every third word flashed in my head like a warning: Situation. Rescue. Chemistry. The quotes around "collaborative chemistry" had all the subtlety of a baseball bat to the ribs. I didn't even bother reading the last line: Hope all is well with you! It was a lie. Chelsea knew it.

There was still that Dropbox link. No title. A mess of numbers and letters: ev-track4-final3.

I wondered if Bishop named it herself, or if Chelsea was trying to keep it anonymous. My jaw was already clamped tight. Didn't even try to smile at the joke. Bishop never used her real name unless she wanted to get under your skin.

I reached for the mouse. Hesitated over the link. For a second, I was eighteen again, hand shaking in the Harmony Heights computer lab, waiting to hear Bishop's demo for the first time. Back then, I thought music could save us both.

Back then, I was an idiot. Clearly.

New tab. Pasted the link, sandboxed it for safety. The download flashed: 31 seconds. Waited. No virus. No drama. Just bytes, moving through fiber, perfectly contained.

I looked down at my hands. Steady, but pale in the blue glare. The skin at the base of my right thumb was raw, old habit from picking at it. I folded both hands in my lap, forced a deep breath, and opened the audio in the DAW. The waveform was a mess: clipped in spots, flat in others, the sort of production that made my inner Virgo want to set the whole hard drive on fire.

Turned the monitors low for the neighbors. Hit play.

Chaos from the jump. The track was "Cathedral." Bishop loved a metaphor you could see coming from three blocks away. Three seconds of dead silence, then a beat that stumbles in, lurching and off grid. The synth sounded like a plastic knife on a toy keyboard. The kick drum, so fat it ate the snare for lunch. Either a rookie mistake or a deliberate "fuck you" to anyone who cared about rhythm.

Then the voice.

It dropped in on the third bar, not on the one, not on any beat that made sense. Didn't even start with a lyric. A laugh. Sharp, wet, the kind you'd rip from a viral Fizzr in a heartbeat. I flinched. Four years since we'd been in the same room, and Bishop could still flip my reptile brain with a single sound.

She started doing something with her voice. Not really singing, not rapping. Declaring. Only Bishop could make that work. The vocals were doubled but out of alignment, like every phrase had an after-shock. She leaned on the vowels, chewed up the consonants, so each line hit like a dare. Six vocal takes at least, all stacked up on the hook, none of them tuned, all drowning in a reverb that clashed with the dry, brittle snare. There was a guitar buried left, but the EQ was so torched it sounded like AM radio underwater.

If anyone else sent me this, I'd have written them off. But Bishop always built traps into her tracks: a fake drop, an intentional fuck-up, something so ugly you had to come closer to figure it out. I knew her games. All of them. That was what you got for being the only person who ever produced her sober.

First verse ended on a line meant to wound. I didn't let myself react. Let it roll into the chorus, where she flipped from minor to major, totally clashing with the chords. Another Bishop move: She wanted harmony to hurt.

At 2:12, she dropped the tempo by ten BPM for a bridge packed with vocals, crowd-thick, gymnasium echo. The words were "let it out," over and over, until they lost all meaning. The compression was pumping, stereo field collapsing. My chest was clenched, hands fisted under the desk, arm burning with old tension I'd thought I'd outgrown.

Kept listening.

Outro: Bishop, raw, "I confess, I confess, I confess"—the reverb bleeding her voice into nothing. I sat back, exhaled, realized I'd been holding in a cringe through the whole track.

Technically, it was a train wreck. The mix was a disaster. Arrangement barely taped together. But the voice? Still a weapon. Bishop was fucking brilliant in the way she flipped metaphors. Wordplay was otherworldly. She spoke about music and creation, art in a way that blew my mind when she was in the zone, but she always needed a buffer for her ideas. Up until years ago, that was me.

My head buzzed. Flexed my fingers, waited for blood to come back. I heard every issue, every fix, every way to Frankenstein it back together until it sounded deliberate. My brain was already working out the session map: The stuttering hi-hat needed quantizing but not to a grid—keep it human. The fake drop would hit harder if the sub-bass was side-chained to the lead. Make the drop out feel like a heart skip. That bridge could start a cappella, then build to a wall, every layer fighting for oxygen.

My hands moved for the faders before I realized. I wasn't touching the board, but my fingers danced in the air, adjusting phantom knobs.

I told myself it was professional curiosity. Doing a solid and running diagnostics for Chelsea. Not because Bishop's sabotage got under my skin. But even as I thought it, I was already leaning forward, hungry for the next trick.

Hit play again. Monitors up, no headphones, no limiter. Let it fill the room and see where the cracks let in air. Elbows on desk, chin in hand, eyes closed to hear every frequency clean.

Final chorus. My heart did its old, stupid kick, half a beat late, bracing for it. I heard her voice slip out of harmony for one phrase, bare and honest for a second. That's what I'd have looped, if we were still working together. What I'd have cut, saved, built the whole thing around.

Slammed the space bar, froze the track mid-echo. Studio was dead again, but the song kept running in my head.

Looked at Chelsea's message. The reply box blinked at me, needy as a dog waiting for a bone.

Closed the email. Dragged the audio to a folder labeled UNSORTED. Shut the laptop with more force than it deserved.

Stood up. Paced a tight circle around the room. Skin hot, prickling, like I'd finished a sprint but couldn't cool off. Went to the kitchenette, dumped the cold coffee, splashed water on my face. My reflection in the steel backsplash looked warped, stretched. I smiled at it anyway. Another trick for breaking the loop.

Back at the board, wiped down the console again. Killed the accent lights, let the room flatten into grayscale. Left the monitors on, because the blue glow reminded me of Harmony Heights nights, waiting for Bishop to send her stems at 2 a.m. while I pretended not to care. I remembered her beside me, feet up on the desk, calling out bad takes with a mouthful of Skittles. Remembered the way she'd email herself notes mid-session, then delete them before I could sneak a look.

Sat back down, just to feel the chair. Loaded up Cam Wolfe's track, played the clean master, and it sounded like nothing. Like glass. I tried Bishop's again, this time through headphones, the way she would have. The first laugh hit me right between the eyes.

"Fuck," I said out loud.

I could fix her sound. But no one ever fixed what broke between us, not even her.

I remembered the first time she stayed over. Not for sex, but because it was 4 a.m. and she was too tired to walk to the subway station. We'd shared my bed like it was nothing, her cold feet finding mine under the covers, both of us scrolling our phones in comfortable silence until we passed out. Woke up with her arm across my stomach and my back pressed against her chest. It was so easy. We were so easy.

When did we lose that?

That thought hit me even harder than hearing her voice did. Harder than the local paper interview we did where she was talking and I was staring at her lips the whole time, dumb in love, thinking she wouldn't notice.

Saved the session, backed up the folder to an encrypted drive. Didn't write Chelsea back. Didn't text Bishop, because that meant unblocking her first. An extra step Past Me put into place to make Future Me really have to mean it enough to break no contact.

Let the silence breathe. The song kept running behind my eyes, behind everything else.

When I finally left the studio, the sky was bleeding into sunrise, and my hands were still mixing.

The Artist At Work, Or Whatever

Bishop

I ONLY STARTED SWEATING after the second fuck-up. Hated when work started feeling like work. Made the gummies wear off a lot quicker.

First time through, bassist missed his entrance by a full bar—*fine*, whatever, 9 a.m. call times are violence against creative people—but then the drummer tripped on a fill I'd specifically marked in sixteenth notes, and by the third botched run my shirt was doing that thing where it sticks to your back in strips. Sweat tunneling down my spine like it had somewhere to be. Disgusting. Iconic. Same thing.

Rehearsal spaces in the city: exposed brick, battered floors, everything smells like a thousand cigarettes and Red Bull had a baby and that baby never showered. Curated as hell. "Authentic" the way a three-hundred-dollar combat boot is authentic—fake as fuck, but visually devastating. The label called this a "stripped-down set," which meant a rented warehouse in Brooklyn, a "neutral color palette," and six thousand dollars' worth of upcycled lighting that was supposed to look accidental. Three days to shoot content for the deluxe reissue. Really, an excuse for me to perform my own existence in front of strangers with good teeth and hidden mics.

It was one of those intimate performance things for the cameras. The kind where you pretend there's no production crew and you're just vibing out with a few friends, except those friends are a million subscribers who streamed your feelings for $10.99 a month.

Biggest performance of my career.

No pressure.

Off to the side, near the folding table loaded with breakfast carbs and cut fruit, a watcher had appeared: a woman in a crisp, pale blue blazer, holding a notebook that looked too expensive for the job. Her shoes were pointed, white and clean enough to get her banned from any real musician's green room. She had that lean-forward energy you only see in journalists and bounty hunters.

Her mouth was set in a permanent smile that didn't reach the eyes. When our gazes locked, she looked down, made a note, then looked up again—almost daring me to come over and read what she'd written.

I looked away. Focused on the band.

"We're gonna stop right there," I said, cutting the song at bar 49. Polite-aggro voice, rehearsal register, bad-sex register. Same frequency. Snare fizzled out. Bassist flinched. Guitarist rolled his eyes at the drummer like he wasn't the one who'd just power-chorded over my vocals for an entire verse.

I exhaled. Hard. "You're early again, Phil. Overblows the guitar."

Drummer Boy—whose actual name was Phil, because of course it was—blinked through the haze, sticks frozen midair like he was posing for a statue nobody asked for. "Sorry, sorry," he said, then louder for the mics, "Got it, Bishop."

"You sure?" I asked, too sweet, like I was offering him poison in a wine glass. "Because if we do it four times in a row it turns into jazz, and I'm not trying to be experimental right now, Phil. I'm trying to not have a public breakdown on camera."

Somebody on the production crew snorted. I risked a glance at the gallery above the glass: four camera operators in black, heads tilted at identical angles, and a photographer with a high-end Fuji and tattooed knuckles stalking the periphery, shooting my anger in twelve frames per second.

I went for the water bottle at the monitor wedge. The label was local, because "realness" was the flavor of the week. I took a long pull of a lukewarm bottle of water I stashed away, swallowing my frustration with the hydration, and let my eyes scan the space.

The only thing in the room that didn't look like a Pixogram set piece was my own fit: thrifted black mesh tank, orange track pants, battered Stan Smiths, and a chain-link belt I'd hot-glued together after a breakdown at two in the morning. I looked like I belonged in a crime scene photo, or a really niche fashion blog.

The field producer was fiddling with her iPad, pretending not to be terrified of me. She wore a navy jumpsuit and kicks that had never seen rain. The assistant director gave me a helpless shrug and made a "reset from top?" gesture, as if I hadn't already resigned myself to another full take.

We played the first verse straight, which was better than I'd expected, but the guitarist (I never learned his name, on principle) managed to play the pre-chorus with a chord progression borrowed from a completely different track. I dropped out, let them finish the train wreck, and then walked to the edge of the stage.

"Pause," I said, loud enough to pop the shotgun mics. "That's not the bridge."

The guitarist looked at me, dead-eyed. "What?"

"You just played the progression from 'Phantasmic,' not 'Overreacting.' "

He made a show of checking his pedalboard, as if the gear was the problem. "Right. Sorry. Got the tracks mixed up."

"Me too," I said, faking a smile. "For a second I thought we were playing to win."

The bassist coughed, but his mouth twitched. Drummer Boy just stared at his hands, already embarrassed. I didn't want to push it. These weren't my real bandmates, just session guys from the label. They played like they had a second gig later tonight, and I respected the hustle, even if it made me slightly homicidal.

But something snagged in my chest. The chord progression he'd played—wrong song, wrong vibe—had sounded better than what I'd written. Cleaner. Like maybe the problem wasn't him forgetting. Maybe the problem was me expecting them to make my messy-ass arrangement make sense.

I shook it off. Grabbed the mic stand harder than I needed to.

"Take five?" the field producer offered. She checked the time on her phone, anxious not to waste daylight, but even more anxious to avoid a full-scale diva meltdown.

"Sure," I said, not meaning it. I walked to the side of the stage, ripped off my in-ear, and wiped the sweat from my temple with the bottom of my tank. The photographer circled, catching every flicker of disgust and annoyance, probably planning the photo spread for a future tell-all.

I made myself stand perfectly still. Let the cameras feast.

I felt the weight of eyes and lenses and expectations. The air was heavy with unsaid things. A guy in a headset fiddled with the light rig, amping it up until the sweat on my collarbones gleamed for the B-roll.

I hated the fake intimacy of these shoots, the way everyone wanted to capture my "process" as if the work was something you could squeeze out of me like a blackhead. Funny thing was, I used to love it. Used to get high off being watched, off turning the making into theater. Now, it just felt like proof I'd forgotten how to do this when no one was looking.

But I'd been doing this since I was sixteen, and the tricks of the trade were hardwired into my DNA: Give them 3 percent more than you wanted, never let the mask drop unless you were ready to burn the room down, and always control the tempo.

I risked a glance to the back of the space. My manager was pacing along the cinderblock wall, phone wedged to his ear. His suit was the same charcoal number he wore to every event. He moved in tight, agitated circles, like a dog circling a patch of grass it didn't want to piss on.

Every so often, his eyes flicked up and caught mine. He gave a small, tight-lipped nod as if he knew I was about to blow my own kneecaps off for content. He'd been managing me since the Harmony Heights days, back when I played to seven people and two of them were just there to take selfies with Shiloh's dad. I wasn't sure if I owed him my loyalty or a formal apology. Probably both.

His voice rose just enough for me to catch a single name. "Shiloh Ellis."

My hand clenched around the water bottle. Plastic crackled.

There. That was the reason I was ready to snap something in half.

The name bloomed inside me like a bruise I forgot I had. For half a second, I caught it—her mouth near my ear, her scent, my hands at her throat, me walking her back into the wall. Her watching me from behind those thick dark frames she always wore. Memory struck fast and burned out faster, and then everything just stopped.

Weird tattoos aside, I'd gotten good at not thinking about it. Most days, anyway.

And they wanted me to work with her again. Have her sitting on the other side of the glass, blank-faced while I performed songs she tore out of me. No biggie.

I forced myself to look away, set my sights on the window instead. A sliver of daylight made it through the grime, turning the dust motes gold. I counted the particles, anything to keep from counting the years since I'd last seen her. My brain, being too damn helpful, correcting "last seen" to "left."

My assistant tapped my shoulder.

"You're up again in two," she said, then lowered her voice. "They want to start the interview segment after this run."

I nodded, still watching my manager pace. He was gesturing now, one hand slicing the air like he could cut through whoever was on the other end of the line.

"Also," she said, quieter, "the label is asking if you're ready to move forward on that conversation. The one they started last week."

My throat tightened. I didn't turn to look at her. Kept my eyes on the window, the dust, the light doing its best impression of hope.

She didn't say "Shiloh," but she didn't have to. The label had been pushing for a new producer since February, the subtext always clear: They wanted someone who could salvage my mess of a second album and maybe, just maybe, salvage me in the process. I knew who they meant the second she said, "move forward."

I took the water bottle she was still holding out, drank half in one go, and made a show of wiping my mouth with my wrist. My fingers were shaking. I balled them into a fist.

"Tell them I'll let them know after lunch."

The assistant hesitated, probably caught in the crossfire between her job and her desire to still be alive by dinner. "It's just..." She trailed off, eyes darting to my manager, then back to me.

I gave her the smile I reserved for preteens and small cats. "You're good," I said. "Thanks."

She nodded, evaporated, and I was alone again.

"Tell them I'm not wearing the hat," I called after her. There was always a hat. Some fuck-awful accessory they wanted to "try" for the press kit. My head was too big, and my hair would just get smooshed underneath.

She grinned over her shoulder, gave a thumbs-up, vanished.

I reset my posture, the tension rose and fell in my shoulders. There was a rhythm to the cycle: performance, collapse, reassemble, repeat.

The reporter in the blue blazer was closer now, pretending to examine the breakfast spread but really just hovering in my periphery. Waiting.

Back on stage, the field producer motioned for me to return. I rolled my shoulders, stomped my feet, tried to walk off the tension before the cameras rolled again.

The director signaled the reset. I could feel the eyes of the world on me—okay, thirty-five people in a Bushwick studio and a growing swarm of virtual fans waiting for the next rumor drop—waiting for the show.

I took my place at center stage, hands on the mic, lips a quarter inch from the mesh. My eyes closed, just for a second, enough to blot out the camera glare and the nerves.

"From the top," I said, soft but direct.

The count-in, then the opening bars, then me. Voice clean, pitch-perfect, with just enough distortion to sound live. The drummer locked in this time, and I let myself ride the groove, just a little. The crowd fed me their familiar hunger that was fuel to my system.

But halfway through the first chorus, the guitarist missed a transition, and my jaw locked, teeth grinding so hard I tasted copper. I didn't show it. I pushed through, a pro to the end, but inside my head I was already dismantling every piece of the set, every piece of myself.

When we hit the outro, I let the beat ride out, all reverb and intention. The sound died, and I stepped back from the mic, heart racing.

I drifted to the other side of the set, biding my time in the shadow of a busted upright piano. It smelled like mildew and ambition, which pretty much summed up the morning so far. The wood was warped, keys yellowed and chipped. Probably hadn't held a tune in years.

I used to be able to make something like this sing.

The thought came and went like a bad lyric. I pushed it down, turned away.

The band clustered around the water table, swapping the universal language of freelance musicians. I pretended not to listen, but my ears were always tuned for insults at a distance.

The reporter with the blue blazer appeared at my side, recorder at the ready.

"Can I ask you something?" she said, voice like she'd learned it in a lab.

I took a breath. Adjusted my stance. Set my face to neutral. "You can try."

She smiled, or maybe just showed teeth. "What's your favorite part about this process?"

I almost laughed. Almost. "The part where it ends."

What I didn't say: I used to live for the middle. The mess, the making, the part where you don't know if it'll break you or make you something holy. Dropped a once-in-a-generation record, made people feel things they didn't have words for, then dipped. Did a whole Frank Ocean, disappeared when the applause was loudest, thinking I could build another cathedral with someone else on organ.

But the magic didn't come back. Not really. The world kept asking where she went, and all I could do was hand them features on other people's songs. Polished, hollow, missing the pulse beneath the mix.

People act like there's some secret ingredient, like the right producer or the right heartbreak can make you immortal. They don't get it. I had the magic. I always have. I can build something out of nothing. Have since I was a kid messing with my parents' instruments. But lately, I can't seem to translate what's in my head, not the way I used to. It's like the signal gets scrambled on the way out. Maybe I lost my edge, or maybe I just need to push harder.

I won't say it's about who was with me back then. That's nostalgia, not science. Shiloh was good, sure. She was the best at catching what I threw out, the only one who could keep up. But this isn't about her. It's about finding my own frequency again. Has to be.

No one would ever say it out loud, not even the reporter with the notebook and the smile like a trap. But there was a moment when it all made sense, and I keep hunting it down, sure I can get back there alone. The part where it ends only hurts if I let myself think too hard about who was standing next to me at the start.

She tapped something on her phone, then just waited, as if silence was an invitation.

"Rough room," she said, at last.

I opened my eyes, adjusted my posture just enough to look casual. "Comes with the territory," I replied. My voice sounded low, flat, like

I'd borrowed it from someone else for the day.

She thumbed the notebook, pretending to scan notes, but really just giving herself something to do with her hands. "Mind if I ask a couple off the record?"

I gave her a look that said there was no such thing, but I nodded anyway. "Sure. Hit me."

She hesitated like she hadn't already written the headline and byline in her head, then said, "Is it true they're bringing in shi.ctrl to, uh, support the next phase of the album?"

Back when we worked together, reporters actually gave a shit about the music. Asked Shiloh technical questions that made her eyes light up as she talked too fast, asked me about lyrics and vision and what we were trying to build. Now, all anyone wanted was the drama. The Harmony Heights studio closing. Who left who and why. Like I hadn't done shit without her, or her without me.

My fingers found the chain-link belt at my hip. Twisted one of the links until the metal bit into my palm.

I took my time.

"You know what's wild?" I said, voice flat. "Y'all used to ask me about music. Now you just want tea."

The reporter blinked, caught.

"Ask the label," I said.

I was already gone, boots hitting pavement, putting bodies and noise between me and whatever bullshit follow-up she had queued up in that notebook.

Peacocking

Shiloh

FIFTEEN MINUTES EARLY. I liked to get eyes on the space before anyone could contaminate it—strip the energy back to zero—then build it up in layers I could control.

The label's main conference room was everything I hated about corporate money: glass walls, glass table, too many awards. You could smell the new carpet and the money trying to hide how new it was—lemon cleaning fluid over mineral tang. Arctic thermostat. Hit you in the lungs.

I wore the gray button-down with cufflinks. Slacks pressed. Watch polished. Hair cut two days ago, fade still sharp. Carrying only essentials: laptop, folder with three annotated copies, notepad, single pen.

Chose the seat second from the head—left side, better angle to the display. Then the ritual: laptop centered, folder stacked, notepad beside it, pen horizontal. Flipped to my notes, underlined key phrases: vocal proximity, dynamic restraint, tempo variance as emotional pivot. I knew what I was going to say but rehearsed the phrasing anyway.

Deep breath. Taste the dry air.

At 8:32, the junior assistant drifted in, set down water and glasses. The A&R came next, handshake already up. I let him hang for a beat before standing.

He launched into industry chatter—Cam Wolfe's numbers, Spotify charts.

I nodded. "Impressive."

The manager rolled in five minutes later. Pinstripe suit, wireless headset, neon green Triple S. He measured the room, took the seat opposite me. We nodded. Mutual respect from the Harmony Heights days. Didn't mention it.

More small talk. Nobody said Bishop's name, but it floated between us anyway, sour and unavoidable.

Then I heard her: boots hitting laminate in that restless *tap-tap-pause*. My pen stopped mid-word. That rhythm—off-beat, impatient, unmistakable. I'd know it in a stadium full of footsteps. The memory was involuntary: How many nights I'd tracked that sound coming down the hall at Harmony Heights, bringing chaos and inspiration in equal measure.

I forced my hand to finish the sentence. Pressed the period hard enough to dent the page.

Then the door swung open.

First impression: trying too hard to show everyone she's the talent. That never changed. Bigger sunglasses sitting on high cheekbones, gradient lens. Blood orange fleece bomber and cropped tee, but the hem was tucked wrong. The joggers were a size too big at the waist, as if she'd bought them for a body she didn't have anymore. Under the bomber she looked collapsed, smaller—leaner in a way that looked intentional. But her arms filled out the sleeves, muscle where softness used to be. Jewelry game was still excessive but not thought through: two different earrings, three chains, none matching the color palette. The tension showed at the collar, the way it bunched against her neck.

Dark circles under the glasses, even though the lenses should've hidden them. Hair was probably styled with the foam brush she kept in her glove compartment at all times. Her hands: nails short, thumb rubbing against the pad like she was already bored or anxious. She floated just inside the doorway, surveying us like a queen checking for traitors.

Three seconds passed. No one said anything.

I shifted in response. Legs spreading slightly, not wide but open, elbows settling heavier on the table. Taking up space the way I'd learned to in rooms full of men who assumed I'd shrink. Old reflex. Bishop peacocks, I anchor. She performs; I ground. We'd always done this dance, even back then. Her energy pulling all the oxygen, mine pulling it back.

The A&R stood up, eager, gesturing to the seat beside him. Bishop didn't move at first—she hovered, hands in her pockets, lips pressed together. Just enough hesitation to hint she'd almost turned around in the hall.

Her eyes flicked to me, past the glasses.

Contact.

Something in me tugged for a second. The same way it used to when she'd look up from a lyric and catch me already watching. I locked it down before it could reach my face.

No smile, no arch of the brow. Just a single nod, sharp and profession-al.

She must've clocked it. Her shoulders braced, just a tiny shift, then she crossed the room and went for her seat. Not the center—never the expected move. She dropped into the chair closest to the window, two down from me, letting her body fold into the angle of the armrest like she was claiming territory.

Silence pulled the tension tighter than an arrow.

The meeting wasn't ready to start, but now everyone was holding their breath anyway. Junior assistant clicked her pen, made a show of adding something to her iPad. The manager kept his hands on his phone, eyes flicking up only once to check if Bishop was settling in.

Bishop adjusted her sunglasses, but behind them I saw the exhaustion in the lines under her frames. For a moment, she reminded me of the old her—back when I'd find her crashed on the battered couch, hoodie pulled over her head, eyes wild and soft at the same time. Always acting like she'd never been vulnerable in her life.

She scanned the room, then let her gaze settle on the middle distance. No words. The mask was on, but it was cracked at the edges.

The A&R executive was a talker. He waited just long enough to see if anyone else would seize the floor, then launched. "Good, everyone's here"—the way you do when you need to reset the temperature.

"First off, thanks to everyone for making the time. We're here because the Bishop project is...at a crossroads. Rollout to date has been high-impact in terms of visibility, but the engagement metrics haven't tracked with projections. We need to course-correct, lean into a coherent narrative, and really define the creative direction as we get this next phase ready for—"

"Public consumption," Bishop finished, deadpan. "Yeah, we got it."

The A&R blinked, smile faltering for half a second. Recovered. The A&R kept talking. Partnership. Synergy. Chemistry.

They didn't know.

To them, we were just two masculine-presenting artists who made good music together. Producer and performer. They saw the short hair, the streetwear, the way we both moved through a room—and stopped looking.

Fine by me.

The label wanted to recreate our "magic." Had no idea what they were actually asking for.

The A&R moved on, faster now. "What really matters is alignment on the vibe for these next sessions. Bishop, you've always thrived in the intersection between chaos and accessibility, but this time we want to see something more...authentic. Maybe a rawer sound, but still with energy. We loved the lead single, don't get me wrong, but we need the album to 'tell a story.' One fans will believe."

Bishop tilted her head. "As opposed to the fake story I've been telling?"

Silence. The assistant's typing stopped. One thing about Bishop was that she knew the problem. She was also the problem.

The A&R's smile went tight. "That's not what I—"

"Nah, nah, I'm genuinely curious." Bishop leaned back, arms crossed. "What part of my life sounds made up to you?"

The manager cleared his throat. Diplomatic rescue attempt. "I think what he means is—"

"... and if we could just get those stems isolated from the first session," the A&R pushed forward, desperate now, "we'll be able to remix on the backend and really amplify the emotional signature without getting lost in post-production chaos—"

I cut in. Didn't bother to look up. "That's not how stem separation works."

The A&R's hand froze mid-gesture. He blinked, recalibrated. "Well, I mean, not literally—but from a workflow standpoint."

"Not from any workflow standpoint." I looked up. They were trying to be cheap about this, have me do a patch job. I didn't work like that. "We'll track clean. Avoid artifacting in the mix. Otherwise, you're paying someone else to fix what I could've done right the first time."

Silence. The A&R's smile went thin.

"And if that's not the project," I said, "I'll have to pass."

Movement in my peripheral. Bishop had been practically horizontal in that chair—hood up, sunglasses on, radiating *I'd rather be anywhere else*. Now, she sat up. Spine straight. The chain at her throat went still.

She didn't say anything. Didn't have to. The room's gravity shifted, everyone suddenly aware that I could end this shit before it started.

The manager nodded quickly. "No, no—of course. Full tracking. Whatever you need."

The label assistant typed it in, word for word.

Bishop settled back, but not all the way. Still watching. "Shiloh doesn't play about her work."

I didn't acknowledge that.

"Shi dot, I'd love your expertise on how we can achieve this sonically. We absolutely want energy—just an evolved form, something that pushes the envelope." He was sweating now, sensing the undercurrent.

I nodded, conceding the point without actually conceding it. "We can drive intensity with arrangement. Doesn't need to be loud to leave a mark."

Manager perked up. "The fans go for honest. If it tracks as real, the numbers will follow."

Bishop's jaw pulled tighter, then let go. I watched the pulse at her neck, how the chain caught the light as she shifted.

She took a breath like she was going to argue, then didn't.

I left the silence open, let it do the work.

Across the table, the label assistant was scribbling on her iPad, capturing every phrase as if it would matter. The A&R softened his tone, pivoting to "shared vision" and "alignment." But between every line, the room was split down the middle—their side, my side, and Bishop stuck in the crossfire.

I underlined my last point, twice, then looked up.

The only thing moving was the second hand on the conference room clock, slicing up the next hour of my life.

I knew the script: reference tracks. The creative team always had a list ready, meant to sound curated but really pulled from whatever algorithm owned their playlist that week.

A&R started with the usual suspects. "Thinking for the up-tempo cuts, maybe lean towards Sable Lake's last album? The singles are streaming huge." He rattled off a few more, all mid-chart, all pre-approved focus group safe.

The manager chimed in. "Cam Wolfe's new stuff with Stacks Monroe is going viral—the critics love how King Ash's production's got that crisp edge but still gives space for their voices."

They both looked at me, waiting for confirmation. I just nodded, made a note on my pad. Under the table, my foot tapped out another odd rhythm. None of these had anything to do with what Bishop needed, but I let them finish.

When the A&R finally exhaled, I reached for my laptop. Didn't say a word until the input cable was clicked, screen mirrored on the wall display, the room's audio system reset to neutral.

"I'd like to add one more reference," I said.

I queued it up from my personal archive. Analog rip, lossless, tagged with a date from when we were kids. The kind of track that never went mainstream because it was too honest, too raw. I shot a glance at Bishop to make sure she was watching—just a quick flick, then back to the screen.

Bishop had written the first verse on my bedroom floor at 2 a.m., half-asleep, scribbling in a composition notebook. I'd built the hook around her humming. She didn't even know I was recording.

The chorus was a prayer. "Let me in while my fists still believe in you."

No tricks in the production. Every flaw was left in, every breath like it hurt to pull in.

Bishop's fingers froze on the table—mid-tap, the motion arrested. For a split second I caught the line of her throat flex as she swallowed, slow and deliberate. Dark lenses stayed on, but her jaw set just a little too hard. She didn't look at me. Didn't look at anyone.

A&R nodded along, oblivious. "This is definitely vibey. Maybe a little lo-fi for Bishop's brand, but the emotionality is what we're after." He typed something on his phone, probably a meeting recap for the label higher-ups.

The manager shrugged, checked his notifications, then scrolled with his thumb. Nobody else in the room heard what I heard.

I let the track run its minute-thirty, then killed the audio. Just enough to shift the room's temperature. Just enough to make sure the subtext was on the table, even if nobody else could name it.

Logistics next. Junior assistant pulled up a calendar, mapped out four months of sessions—sometimes three a week. Knowing us, some would be all-nighters. The A&R stressed "overlap for flexibility," "organic workflow," "capture lightning in a bottle." I didn't argue. Just nodded. Underlined my deliverables and left the rest to the suits.

"Shiloh, you're comfortable with that?" A&R asked.

"Yes," I said.

He brightened. Pivoted to Bishop, but she just nodded, barely moving her head. Still locked on a spot over his shoulder, somewhere past the glass.

"Great," he said, clapping his hands together. "I think the synergy between you two is going to unlock something truly special. It'll be an extremely collaborative process—" He pushed his palms outward, like literally shaping air between Bishop and me.

Manager offered a thin smile. Bishop didn't react. She was all poker face, but if you looked close, her breathing was too measured, too careful. Hands folded on the table, chain bracelets twisted tight at the wrist.

The reference track kept playing in my head. I wondered if she heard it, too.

They started hashing out non-disclosure language, project milestones, the legalese nobody but the lawyers would ever read. I tuned out, made another note, shut my eyes for a second to feel the last echo of the song. It clung to the inside of my skull, bittersweet and sticky.

At the far end of the table, Bishop sat like a statue, sunglasses trained on the artfully distressed wall as if it might open up and swallow her whole. Maybe it was better that I couldn't see the eyes behind them.

The air, already cold, got just a little colder.

Last item was personnel. The A&R twisted in his chair. "Let's talk session players. We want the best, but keep it lean."

I was ready. From the folder, I slid out the shortlist: five names, all ringers, explained why I wanted this crew.

Noted. Didn't comment. Not even a blink.

I finished the list, methodical. "If we need any external vocals, I'll source from the alumni pool. Skye Bella's available—I checked her schedule yesterday. She'd fit the textural gaps. No outside producers, no background hands."

Bishop sat up straighter. "Not Skye."

I paused, pen hovering. "Why not? You've worked with her before—"

"Just—no." Her jaw set. "She's busy. And her vibe's wrong for this."

"She's not busy. I literally just said I checked."

"Well, maybe I don't want to work with her." Bishop's voice went flat, defensive. "That cool with you, or do I not get a say?"

The assistant stopped typing. The A&R suddenly found his phone very interesting.

I looked at Bishop. Something was off. *That* reaction was too big, too fast.

"It's your album," I said quietly. "No Skye."

I crossed her name off the list. Drew the line slow, deliberate.

Bishop looked away first.

A&R looked like he swallowed a bee. "Perfect. That's the mix of fresh and familiar we want to see." He spun to the calendar, tapped a few keys. "I'll have Chelsea lock in contracts—first deliverable two weeks out, final edits by end of six. Sound right?"

"Yep," I said.

Paper shuffling. Junior label assistant rounded up her iPad, phone, and a sleeve of business cards she hadn't handed out. The manager scooped up his phone, put in a call without leaving the table, muttering logistics into the ether. I closed the laptop—deliberate, with a muted click—then lined it up in my messenger bag, followed by notepad, pen. Nothing left behind.

The chairs scraped against the floor, one after another. None of them designed for comfort, just for effect. The A&R was already halfway to the door, calling instructions over his shoulder: "Chelsea will get you the new reference playlist, and Bishop, your promo obligations are cut back for the next cycle—focus on the music."

Her sunglasses never moved. She just nodded, barely.

I reached for the strap of my bag, checked my pocket for the watch.

Time to go.

I stood. Bishop was still in her chair, statue-perfect, but her attention had shifted, almost as if she was waiting on a cue.

First step toward the door, and I heard it:

"Shiloh."

Voice wasn't stage volume. Softer, almost private. I stopped, one hand on the back of my chair, pivoted to face her.

The room was already empty except for us. Fluorescent hum, the scuff of a rolling chair somewhere down the hall.

She hesitated. For a split second, she looked less like Bishop, more like the girl who used to huddle in the studio at 2 a.m., asking questions she already knew the answers to.

"The studio on West Sixth—is that where we'll be tracking?" she said.

It was right there in the project brief she'd been handed an hour ago, page two, top of the sheet. She asked anyway.

I held her eyes, let the silence ring for three seconds, just to see if she'd flinch.

"Yes," I said. "Nine a.m. Monday."

She nodded, jaw tight. The chain at her throat trembled, just once.

The moment ran out, then I turned and walked. Tried not to run.

Click, Gone
Bishop

FIRST THING I CLOCKED: the setup had evolved. More gear everywhere, cables in organized chaos, Shiloh's analog desk now sprouting
outboard preamps. It looked less like a church, more like a crime scene.
With Funko Pops.

Second thing: people. Three session musicians already set up, none of
whom I recognized. Parker on drums, coral buzz cut. Mar on bass,
built solid. Ian on keys, older, setting up a fortress of synths.

Shiloh was behind the glass in the control room, looking down at a
mixing board, hands moving with a confidence that made you think
she was born plugged in. She wore a navy shirt, sleeves rolled to the
elbow, curls cut even shorter than at the meeting, like she'd gone home
and shed the last of her patience with the world. Skin the color of

peanut butter, smooth and warm under the studio lights. The kind I used to trace in the dark, mapping constellations I'd never admit I memorized. For a beat, she didn't look up. Then she did—a glance, nothing more, but it felt like a laser. She held the look just long enough for me to get the message: Not now.

I pasted on a smile and breezed past the musicians into the room.

The control room was separated by a thick pane of glass. I'd spent enough nights on the other side, watching her face for signs of approval, waiting for her to say into the mic "good" or "again." I walked in without knocking.

Shiloh didn't turn around. "You're early," she said, voice low but precise.

I dropped my bag on the battered couch. "So are you. Didn't think you'd let anyone else touch your setup."

"Efficiency," she said. "Deadline is non-negotiable." She flicked a fader with her thumb, made a note in the margin of a spiral notebook. She had three notebooks stacked, all identical except for the color-coded tape at the spine.

I stretched, casual. "Missed you too."

Her jaw worked, grinding once. "Did you read the production email?"

" 'Attached: preliminary plan, session schedule, gear list, personnel.' You always did love a bullet point."

"It's all in there." Very, I said what the fuck I said.

I looked through the glass at the musicians. "Whose idea was that crew?"

She kept her eyes on the monitor. "Mine. You need a rhythm section that can read your tempo changes in real time. And you always said you hated tracking with software drums."

I grinned. "That's true. Who's paying them?"

"Label. You're recoupable." She finally turned, eyes dead level with mine. "We're tracking 'Phantasmic' first. The chart is on the stand."

I crossed my arms, leaned against the patch bay. "Didn't realize we were demoing with an audience."

She shrugged. "They're here for your benefit, not theirs. Unless you want to run it solo first?"

I thought about saying yes, just to make a point. But my heart was pounding with something that felt suspiciously like anticipation. This was what I'd been itching for: The chance to show everyone I still had that heat, even if I had to do it in front of strangers.

Instead, I played it chill. "Let's see if they can hang."

The session musicians were bantering when I walked back in. Parker had the stutter-step cadence of a kid who'd gone to music school but never got the accent knocked out of him. Mar kept time with the toe of her boot even when she wasn't playing. Ian nodded, nothing else, like that should be enough. I respected that.

Shiloh piped in over the intercom, her voice bright and public. "Ready for soundcheck?"

Parker gave a thumbs-up, then ran a quick paradiddle just to show off. It was annoyingly clean.

I set my water bottle on the amp, straightened my chain, and checked the mic. "Levels are good?"

Shiloh's voice: "Levels are perfect."

I made a show of reviewing the chart. Then I tossed it onto the floor, shrugged, and said, "Let's just try it cold."

Parker counted us in, and on the downbeat, everything snapped into place. For the first four bars, it felt tight—almost too tight. Like a suit you'd bought for a wedding but never tailored. But when the verse landed, the old engine kicked in: my voice bending around the beat, the band following just behind, every note a little heavier than it needed to be.

Shiloh's face behind the glass didn't move. Not even when I punched the chorus up an octave or let the bridge hang in the air just half a bar longer than was written. But I saw her hand, ghosting over the faders, tracking every move.

We made it to the last chorus, held the final note, let it drop.

Parker laughed. "That was sick."

Shiloh clicked the talkback. "Run it again. Tighter on the bridge."

Not a request. A command.

We ran it multiple times. Each take, I pushed harder—vocal runs that weren't in the chart, tempo shifts that forced the band to chase me. By the last one, I was inventing harmonies on the fly. Shiloh recorded everything. Said nothing.

〜〜〜📶〜〜〜

After lunch, I was buzzing. First day back with Shiloh, and it didn't completely suck. The band was tight, my voice felt good, and for once I wasn't the chaos gremlin fucking up everyone's workflow.

I grabbed my water and headed back to the booth, ready for round two.

Shiloh was already at the console, headphones on, scrolling through the morning's takes. I knocked on the glass. She held up one fin-ger—wait.

I waited.

She pulled off the headphones and gestured for me to come in.

"What's up?" I leaned against the doorframe, trying to read her face.

"Sit." Not a request.

I sat.

She pulled up the track. The one I'd been proud of. The one where I'd layered this perfect field recording underneath the kick: crickets and

47

distant traffic, all grainy and textured. I'd recorded it outside Harmony Heights years ago, spent three weeks getting the EQ just right so it sat under everything like a secret.

She played it back. Through the monitors, it sounded exactly how I wanted: organic, lived-in, real.

"This." She pointed at the waveform. The track with my field recording, barely visible under the drums. "What is it?"

"Atmosphere," I said, defensive already. "Texture. It's a recording I made outside Harmony, back when—" I stopped. Didn't need to finish that sentence. "It adds depth."

"It adds mud." She soloed just the beat—no field recording.

The difference was immediate. The kick punched harder. The hi-hats sat higher in the mix. Everything sounded...expensive. Clean. Professional.

Like every other fucking track on the radio.

I waited for her to cave. Old Shiloh would've played both versions, asked which one I liked better, then kept whichever one made me happy. Old Shiloh treated my artistic vision like gospel, even when I was clearly on my bullshit.

This Shiloh just looked at me.

"See?" She said it like a teacher waiting for me to figure out the answer. "You've got all this low-mid information fighting with the bass. The 'texture' is just clouding everything."

My jaw tightened. "That's the point. It's supposed to feel organic. Real. Not like—" I gestured at the pristine mix. "—a fucking car commercial."

"You think grime makes it authentic?" No judgment in her voice. Just a question.

"I think polish makes it boring."

She nodded, like she'd expected that. "Okay. So explain the lyric to me. The second verse. What are you actually saying?"

I blinked. "What?"

"The lyrics. 'Stained glass boys with the mismatch fit/Look like chaos, walk like a myth.' What's that about?"

"Fashion crimes," I said, grinning. "It's a public service announcement about mixing patterns."

Shiloh didn't smile. Just waited.

"I don't know, man. It's just a vibe. Wordplay." I shrugged, trying to make it nothing. "Sounds cool, that's all that matters."

"That's all?"

"Yeah. That's all."

"Right." She played just my vocal, isolated.

She added the field recording back in.

"And when I listen to this—" The clarity muddied. My voice got buried. "—all I hear is you hiding. Adding dirt so people can't get too close to what you're actually saying."

I had on a screw face, but she was right. Of course she was right.

The old Shiloh would've stopped there. Would've said "but it's your call" and kept the sample because I wanted it.

This Shiloh leaned forward. "Four years ago, I would've left it in. I would've told myself you knew best, that my job was just to make your vision sound good. And you know what happened? You made an album that sounded exactly like what you thought you wanted. And then I got Chelsea asking me to fix it."

Fuck.

"I'm not doing that again," she said. Voice steady. Certain. "My job isn't to be your 'yes woman.' It's to make you sound like the best version of yourself. Even when that means telling you no."

I stared at the waveform. All those hours of work.

"That sample took me three weeks to get right," I said, quieter.

"I know." She wasn't being cruel. Just honest. "And it's a beautiful sample. But it's not serving the song."

She moved the cursor to the delete key. Didn't click yet.

"Your call," she said. "But if you want me to produce this album—actually produce it, not just record whatever you hand me—then you have to trust that I'm hearing something you're not."

I stared at her. The old Shiloh used to apologize when she disagreed with me. Used to soften every note with "maybe" and "just a thought." This Shiloh sat with her hand on the mouse, waiting. No apology. No hedging. Just confidence.

I stared at the waveform. All those hours of work. My hands twisted in my shirt hem.

"Four years ago, you would've kept it," I said. Not angry. Just...tired. "You would've kept it because I wanted it."

"And we both know how that turned out." She moved the cursor. "So are we doing this differently or not?"

The words hit like a slap. I looked away.

"You had your dad's studio," I said finally. Couldn't look at her. "I had one shot."

Silence. Heavy enough to drown in.

Shiloh's jaw worked. When she spoke, her voice was careful. Controlled. "I know."

"Do you?" I turned back to face her. "Because from where I was sitting, you had options. You could fail and try again. I couldn't. So yeah, I took the deal. I took the deal that said I was the magic, not us. And I tried to make it work alone and I couldn't, and now I'm back here asking you to save me again, and I fucking hate that."

Her hand dropped from the mouse.

"This isn't about saving you," she said. Steady. Sure. "This is about you finally trusting yourself enough to let someone help."

"Delete it," I said.

"You sure?"

"Yeah." I swallowed hard. "You're right. It's armor. And I'm—" I gestured helplessly. "—I'm trying to do the thing where I'm not hiding anymore. So. Yeah. Delete it."

She held my gaze for a second. Then clicked.

The stem disappeared.

She played the beat back. Clean. Clear. My voice fully exposed.

"Fuck," I breathed. "That's actually—"

"Better." Not gloating. Just stating fact. "And scarier."

"Yeah." I slumped back in the chair. "A lot scarier."

She saved the session. "Good. That's the whole point." She stood, grabbed her notebook. "We're tracking 'Invasive Species' next. And Bishop?"

"Yeah?"

"No more hiding. If I catch you burying the good stuff under bullshit again, I'm calling you out every time. That's the deal."

I should've been mad. Should've felt attacked, micromanaged, stripped of my artistic vision.

Instead, I just felt...paper thin. Read cover to cover.

"When did you get so bossy?" I tried to make it a joke.

She almost smiled. "When I realized being nice was just another way of lying."

The band was good, but the arrangements felt safe. Predictable. Not me.

By the time we hit "Invasive Species" I'd had enough.

We ran the bridge four times. Every time, I hated it more. Too clean. Too normal.

On the fifth try, I ripped off the headphones mid-take.

"Pause."

In the control room, Shiloh froze.

I paced in front of the drum kit, snapping my fingers. "Can we try something?"

Mar looked wary. "What are you thinking?"

"The bridge needs to stutter. Like you're about to trip but you catch yourself." I beatboxed it, ugly and raw. "Dun-dun—*rest*—dun-dun-dun—"

Parker started tapping his knee, not getting it.

Ian perked up. "Dotted eighths, rest on the downbeat?"

"Exactly. But weirder. Like I'm wrestling the song and sometimes the song wins."

Shiloh's voice over the intercom: "You want a push-pull?"

"*Yes.*" Finally, she was hearing me.

Parker ran it—snare barely grazing the two, then a fat flam on the next bar. The whole thing jerked forward, stopped dead, launched again.

I demoed it once. Twice. The band fought me the first time, followed the second. By the third run, it felt *alive*.

Shiloh's finger hovered over record. She pressed it.

We did the bridge again, crashed the final chord. I staggered back, breathing hard.

Silence.

Mar whistled, low. "That's fucked-up. In a good way."

Parker nodded. "That's a signature move."

I wiped sweat from my forehead, grinning. Looked at the control room, waiting.

Shiloh had her arms folded, head tilted. For a second, I thought she'd say nothing.

Then, into the mic: "Take five. Keep that arrangement. That's the record."

No "good job." No compliment.

But I heard it in her voice—she felt it too.

By the time we wrapped, the sun had burned out. Parker packed up first, gave me a real nod of respect. "That was next-level, Bishop."

Mar handed me a card with her Pixogram. "If you ever need a bassist, I'm there."

Ian just left, ghost-like.

I should've left too. But I hung around the live room, pacing, trying to bleed off the high. I heard Shiloh through the glass, talking to herself, annotating the session.

When the last footsteps faded, I drifted into the control room.

Shiloh was coiled around her work—mouse darting, notebook filling, shoulders hunched like she was building a wall.

I dropped into the chair next to the console.

Waited.

She didn't look up.

I waited longer, just because I could.

Finally, she killed the monitor volume. Glanced over, eyes rimmed dark through dark frames.

"Good session."

I tried a joke. "I only melted down twice. That's progress."

She almost smiled, then she turned back to the screen, started comping takes.

"So," I said, leaning in. "What's the verdict?"

Close enough to see where her fade met skin. Close enough that if I breathed deep, I'd get a hit of that Shiloh scent that was like drugs to my nervous system.

Her hands stopped moving. Froze mid-reach for the mouse, like I'd said something in a language she had to translate first.

She clicked my stuttered bridge, replayed it. "Mix is dense. Lot of artifacts. You're pushing the preamp too hard, but I can dial it back."

"No, I mean—" I stopped, hating how needy I sounded. "Did it work? The bridge thing?"

She isolated my vocal, played it raw. Every breath sounded like a threat. She looped it. "It's different. I think it's better. I'll know tomorrow."

I was still leaning in, close enough to clock the tension in her jaw. Close enough that when she stood up—sudden, like she'd just remembered something urgent—I caught myself halfway out of my chair, body already trying to follow before my brain could tell it to chill the fuck out.

She crossed to the cable rack, started wrapping. Meticulous, almost too hard. Everything about her was controlled. It made me want to break something.

"You never say if you *like* it."

She paused, cables coiled in hand. "Does it matter?"

"It does to me."

Her throat worked. I clocked it in real time: the slow swallow, the way her fingers tightened around the cables until her knuckles went pale. She didn't move. Didn't breathe.

She met my eyes. For maybe two seconds, the Shiloh I remembered looked back—the one who'd stay up till 4 a.m. because we were *this close* to getting it right. The one who used to grin at me when we pulled off something nobody else would've tried.

Then she blinked and it was gone.

"We're not sixteen anymore," she said, returning to her gear. "What matters is the work."

My stomach dropped. Not even dropped—fell hard, a whole missed step in the dark.

I thought if we just made good music together, that would be enough. That I could prove myself through the work, and we'd build back from there without having to actually dig into everything I fucked up. No big conversations, no accountability—just let the sessions speak for themselves until one day she'd look at me like she used to.

My typical brand of bullshit. Perform my way out of the hard part.

I wanted to tell her the work was me. That every fucked-up thing I sang into that mic was just me trying to say "see me, know me, remember what we had" in a way she might actually hear.

But maybe she was telling the truth. Maybe all that mattered to her now was the work.

And that was worse than anything else she could've said.

I shrugged, big and exaggerated, hands spread like *whatever*. Backed toward the door, all loose limbs and easy smile. "See you tomorrow, then."

She kept working. Coiling cables with those precise movements, humming something under her breath—probably already thinking about tomorrow's session, already three steps ahead.

My chest got tight. Like I was being shut out of a room I used to have a key to.

"See you at nine?"

She glanced back. Barely. "Yup."

Cool. Professional as hell, like she's talking to another artist on her roster.

Like we'd never been anything else.

I walked to my truck. The cool air sliced through my sweatshirt. The lot was mostly empty. I climbed in, slammed the door too hard.

Didn't start the engine. Didn't move.

My hands were all twitchy, but it wasn't nerves. Just the usual post-session bullshit. Adrenaline with nowhere to go, brain replaying every moment, picking apart what worked and what didn't.

But there was also something else. Something that made me want to walk back in there, bang on the studio door, make her say it—make her admit the session was good, that I was good, that she felt something when we worked together.

She'd deleted my sample. Just—*click*—gone. Three weeks of work vanished like it never existed. And the fucked-up part? The song was better without it.

We used to have this thing where we'd rate mixes on a scale of "gas station sushi" to "your grandma's cooking." Everything was a food metaphor. Now it's just "sounds good" or "needs work."

My head fell back against the headrest. I did nothing but breathe and try not to think about all the shit I'd never say out loud.

When I finally started the car, the dash lit up sickly orange. I took the long way home, letting the city's empty grid unwind. Stopped for tacos from that truck I found last time.

Somewhere in my head, the bridge riffed on repeat—all stutter and heat, proof I could still pull miracles out of thin air.

Tomorrow, I'd come back and do it again.

Maybe this time, she'd look at me the way she used to.

Or maybe I'd finally get the message.

Pretend We're Not Here

Shiloh

The email from Chelsea came in last night.

Documentary crew arriving at 10 for promo footage. Should only take 2-3 hours. Full cooperation appreciated.

I blinked at my phone, coffee going cold in my hand.

A documentary crew. In my studio. Filming while we worked.

Everything in me wanted to cancel. Make up an equipment failure, a scheduling conflict, anything. But this was label-mandated, part of the album rollout. Bishop's face would be plastered on billboards soon enough—they needed behind-the-scenes content to sell the "creative process" to appease the messy folks who wanted to see us in each other's space again.

I texted back:

Confirmed.

My hands started itching before I even swiped my badge.

Jinx and I spent the next two hours prepping: gear check, session files organized, cables routed and labeled so nothing would go wrong on camera. Control. If I controlled every variable, I could get through this.

The session musicians arrived at 8:30—Parker, Mar, and Ian again. I'd called them back for another day of tracking. They set up efficiently, used to the routine now.

Bishop arrived shortly after, but earlier than usual. She clocked my energy immediately—the too-neat cable coils, the color-coded notebook open to a blank page, my shoulders already up.

"Crew's coming today?" she asked.

"Ten o'clock."

She nodded, dropped her bag on the couch. Didn't make a joke about it. Didn't ask if I was okay.

Just: "We'll make it quick."

The crew showed up at 10:15—director, PA, camera operator, sound tech. Four people, plus lights, plus equipment cases that took up half the control room. The director introduced himself, shook our hands too long, explained the vision: raw, authentic, capturing the magic of collaboration.

"We'll just be flies on the wall," he said. "Pretend we're not here."

Impossible. They were *everywhere*. The PA adjusting boom mics over my head. The camera operator circling the console, lens six inches from my hands. The director asking questions between every take:

"What are you hearing?"

"How do you know when it's right?"

"Can you explain that technical term?"

In the live room, the band ran through their parts. Parker kept rhythm even during the interruptions, Mar tuned between takes, Ian adjusted his synth patches. They seemed unbothered by the cameras. Professional.

Bishop handled it fine too. Smiled at the camera, made jokes, explained her process like she'd done this a hundred times. Performed.

I answered when spoken to. Kept my responses short. Tried to focus on the work.

But my shoulders crept higher. My answers got shorter. The music we were tracking sounded stiff, lifeless—everything squeezed out by the performance of making it.

We gathered at the corner of the control room. The crew closed in with cameras and lights.

"Can we get that one more time? The lighting wasn't quite right."

I bit down on the inside of my cheek. We'd already run this section four times. The take was fine. Better than fine.

"Sure," I said. Flat.

Bishop was in the booth, headphones half-off, waiting. She caught my eye through the glass, eyebrow raised.

I cued the track again.

The documentary crew had been here for two hours. What was supposed to be "unobtrusive B-roll" had turned into a full production—lights repositioned every ten minutes, the PA constantly adjusting boom mics, the director asking us to "run that section again but with more energy."

My shoulders damn near up to my ears. Every time I reached for a fader, someone's reflection moved in the monitor glass. Every time I tried to focus, someone asked a question about my "creative process" or "collaborative dynamic."

The session was dying. I could hear it in the takes—stiff, overworked, the life squeezed out.

We wrapped the song. The director clapped his hands together. "Great! Now, before we get more tracking, let's do a quick interview segment. Just a few questions about the project."

I wanted to say no. Wanted to tell them we were behind schedule, that we needed to work. But Chelsea had made it clear—full cooperation with the promo team.

"Sure," I said again.

The director smiled at Bishop. "Walk us through your creative process for this album. Where do the ideas come from?"

Bishop leaned back, casual. "Life, mostly. You write what you know, right? Sometimes that's a feeling, sometimes it's a person. Sometimes it's just—" She gestured vaguely. "—trying to figure out what the fuck happened and why it still matters."

The director nodded, eating it up. Turned to me. "Shi dot, you're working with Bishop again after—what, four years? How does it feel being back in the studio together?"

My jaw clenched. "It's good. We have a history. Makes the work easier."

"The chemistry is pretty undeniable," the director pressed. "You two seem to have a real creative synergy."

Chemistry. Synergy. Safe words for something that felt nothing like safe.

"We know each other's process," I said, giving nothing.

Bishop shifted beside me. I didn't look at her.

If one of us had been femme, he would've asked different questions. Would've seen what was actually there instead of "creative synergy."

But we were both illegible to him. Just collaborators. Just profession-
als.

Fifteen years of romantic mess, reduced to good working chemistry.

The director moved on to technical questions—gear, timeline, influ-
ences. I answered on autopilot, counting down the seconds until this
was over.

"One more thing," the PA said. "Can we get a shot of the two of you
working together? Maybe share headphones at the desk, look at the
track?"

My stomach dropped. These weren't even meant for mixing dual
channel, had too much reverb and static. Missed everything in the
other ear. But they were aiming for messy, I guess.

Sharing headphones meant proximity. Meant her shoulder against
mine, her breath near my neck, her body heat in my space. Meant
pretending that was normal, professional, nothing.

I focused on the headphones on the console.

The director smiled. "Just for B-roll. Won't take a minute."

Bishop grabbed the left can, held it out. Our eyes met. She knew. I
peeped it in the way her jaw set, the challenge in her expression.

I took the right can. My fingers accidentally touched hers.

We positioned ourselves at the console. I pulled up a random section
of timeline, didn't even look at what it was. Bishop leaned in to see the

screen. Her shoulder hovered against mine—solid, warm, too familiar. I smelled her cologne. Something new for her.

My jaw locked. Teeth grinding so hard I tasted copper.

"Point at something on the screen," the director said. "Make it natural."

Natural. Right.

I pointed at a waveform. "This section needs tightening."

Bishop leaned closer to look. Her shoulder crushed mine. She cleared her throat. "Where?"

Contact. My whole body went stiff. The cameras were rolling and I had nowhere to put this. Couldn't lean in, couldn't pull away without them clocking everything.

Gravity is meant to pull, isn't it? So I stayed rigid.

"There." My voice came out rough.

"Got it!" the director said. "Perfect chemistry, you two."

Bishop looked at me like she'd forgotten we had an audience. The cold air rushed in where her warmth had been.

I put down the headphones, crossed back to the other side of the console. Put the desk between us.

The director checked his watch. "Okay, let's get one more song tracked before we lose the light. Shi dot, can you walk us through your board setup while the band gets ready?"

No. No, I couldn't. I needed them gone. Needed to breathe without someone watching, needed to work without performing, needed—

Bishop stood up. "Actually, you should check out the live room first. The way Jinx set up the drum mics? That's the real art."

The director perked up.

Bishop headed for the door, beckoning them to follow. "Come on, I'll show you. Most people just throw overheads directly over the kit, but he angles them to catch the room's reflection. Makes the drums sound huge without losing definition. And see how he's got the kick mic just off axis? That's why the low end doesn't turn into mud when we layer..."

Her voice faded as she led them into the live room, hands gesturing at the mic stands, pulling their focus completely.

The director's eyes went wide. "We need to get this on camera. The technical artistry angle—"

"Exactly," Bishop said. "People think it's all about the performance, but half the magic is in the setup."

In less than a minute, she had the whole crew clustered around the drum kit, the PA filming mic positions, the director asking questions about signal chain.

The control room went quiet.

Just me and the console and the faint murmur of voices through the glass.

I could breathe again.

The camera crew had apparently gotten what they wanted, so they started talking among themselves and, most importantly, leaving me the fuck alone.

Bishop drifted back into the control room. She didn't say anything at first, just leaned over the console and listened to the playback. Her body language was soft, the tension gone.

I queued up the take, ran it back from the top. She closed her eyes, nodded along, her foot tapping the beat. When it finished, she looked at me sideways and said, "You ever wonder if we're just remixing the same three minutes of our lives, over and over?"

I thought about it. "Maybe that's all art is. Finding new ways to loop the thing that broke you."

She winced. I winced.

Neither of us said anything else.

The crew was packing up. The studio musicians loaded gear and said quick goodbyes. Bishop went to the couch, sprawled out with a notebook in her lap, scribbling.

I stayed behind the console, organizing tomorrow's session files. Pulled up the day's takes. Started logging timecodes for the edit.

In the monitor's reflection, Bishop was behind me. Pen moving fast across the page. Heavy eyebrows pulled together in concentration.

I looked back at the screen. Flagged a section that needed comping.

Glanced up again. Bishop had stopped writing, was chewing the end of her pen, staring at nothing.

Back to the timeline. Adjusted a fade.

Up again. She was writing now, faster, almost frantic.

I forced my eyes down. Kept them there.

After the last case was rolled out and the director gave his double-cheek air kisses, the space went still. Like someone had vacuumed the room of all sound but the cooling tick of the amps. I'd never realized how many hours of my life were spent listening to machines power down.

Bishop had her shoes off, feet in socks tucked under her on the couch, spiral notebook balanced on one knee. She watched the door as it latched, then let her head fall back before scribbling some more. For a few breaths, neither of us moved.

The black tank top pulled across shoulders that had broadened since I'd seen her last. Her arms had definition now—clean lines from shoulder to elbow, the kind that came from use, not performance. When she shifted to write, her bicep flexed without her meaning to, and my gaze dropped to her forearm, the tendons shifting under skin as her hand moved across the page. I turned back to my desk before I could catalog anything else. My mouth dried right up.

I checked the console. There was nothing left to do. The take was perfect, the files auto-backed to two drives and the cloud. My hands stilled on the exciter app, wanting a job, but the only thing left was to turn the room dark and go home.

Still didn't move.

This time, she looked up. Rolled her shoulders, let them drop. "They really did a number on you."

"It's fine. I'm used to it."

"You shouldn't have to be." Her voice was soft. The type of gentle that set off screaming alarms.

I stared at the screen, blinking at the cursor in the session notes.

For a while, the silence held. I felt her looking at me, waiting for the signal.

So I gave it, even though my throat tried to close up on the words. "Thanks. For handling them."

She made a noise—dismissive, almost a scoff. "They were fucking up the vibe. Couldn't get a clean take with someone breathing down your neck every five seconds."

Casual. Easy. As if it had been about the music and nothing else.

But the take we'd already captured was fine. Better than fine.

I turned back to the screen, jaw tight. Started organizing files I'd already organized. Anything to not look at her.

"I'll send the bounce by morning," I said.

"Cool."

She was still there. Still in the room, almost hesitating. Was she waiting for something? If so, what?

Her hand was on the doorframe. Fingers pressed against the wood as if she was holding herself in place. Or holding herself back.

"See you Thursday," she said finally, before heading out. The door clicked shut.

I sat in the silence, hands flat on the console. Finally, all those people out of my space.

Bishop had protected me. Read me. Remembered exactly what I needed and how to give it to me without making it *a thing*.

The same way she used to at Harmony Heights—checking if I'd eaten, kicking people out when sessions got too loud, knowing when I needed space before I knew it myself.

I'd almost melted over that. Over basic human decency. Over her doing the bare minimum of noticing I was uncomfortable and acting on it.

Pathetic.

I had learned to exist without her, and one redirect of a camera crew had me ready to crack open.

I shut down the console. Grabbed my bag and locked up.

The entire drive home, I kept my hands at ten and two, breathing steady, telling myself this changed nothing.

The radio had come on with the ignition—some soft R&B thing, all breathy vocals and gentle production. I punched the preset. Led Zeppelin flicked to life, drums, muscular bass and screaming guitar.

Better.

Starting Over, And Other Misheard Lyrics

Bishop

ALMOST TWO MONTHS OF working with her again. Six tracks laid down. Just the biggest ones left.

I got there at 9:18, exactly nineteen minutes late, which was a personal best for me considering I'd been sitting in my car outside for thirty minutes having a full spiral. By the time I reached the basement, my palms were already damp, and I'd forgotten the opening line I'd spent all morning rehearsing—something casual, something that didn't sound like I'd been thinking about her hands on that mouse for weeks. Those hands. The ones that knew every inch of me.

"Come in." Shiloh's voice, flat and certain.

I pushed through. She stood near the console wearing her typical uniform: black band tee, jeans, Docs. No jewelry, just the watch at her left wrist. The lavender was stronger in here, the real stuff, and it hit me like a memory I never agreed to keep.

She didn't say anything right away. Just stepped aside, letting me through. I tried to walk in like I owned the place, but my boots stuck on the threshold, catching on a loose strip of door tape. Smooth. The air was cold, dry, recycled five times before it hit the lungs.

Shiloh gestured to the main console. "You want water, tea?"

I shook my head. "I'm good."

She dropped into the desk chair, spun it a quarter turn. "You can sit. Wherever." She was already reaching for the power on the main board.

I picked the high stool by the wall, farthest from the console, and tried to fold myself into the smallest possible shape without looking like I was shrinking.

"So," I said, spinning my left ring like a nervous rosary, "you got the Dropbox?"

Shiloh nodded. "Three versions. I compared them, ran the files through a clean chain so nothing would get flagged in the stems." She clicked through a rapid sequence—she always did everything at triple speed in the morning—more machine than woman. "Want to play it back from the top?"

"Let's do it." My voice broke on the "do," so I covered it by adjusting my jacket—blue today, vintage but not the original, just a well-aged knockoff.

She started the playback. The monitors hissed, then the demo rolled out—my demo, my voice doubled and buried in its own effect chain, fighting for space with a synth line that was too busy by half. I stumbled over every missed beat, every flat note, every decision I made to be "edgy" that now just sounded unfinished.

Shiloh leaned forward, elbows on knees, listening with the focus of a crime scene investigator. She didn't move the whole time. Not a blink.

I tried to look casual, but my leg kept bouncing against the metal base of the stool.

When the track ended, I exhaled like I'd just run a lap. The silence after was twice as loud as the song.

Shiloh spoke first. She looked right at me, through me. "You're not committing to any of the ideas. It's like you wanted to do five different things and did all of them halfway. It's not messy enough to sound intentional and not clean enough to be commercial." She tilted her head. "Which is weird, because you're usually good at living in the mess."

Heat warmed my ears in a way that made me shrink. My fingers pinched the web between thumb and forefinger until it hurt. "Wow, tell me how you really feel," I said, and immediately regretted it. I sounded like a child in a Pixogram fight.

Shiloh's face didn't move. "You asked."

I looked at the gear, at the little tape flags she'd used to label the faders. One of them had my name on it from the last session we ever did, still in the same blue Sharpie.

I made myself laugh. "You ever think maybe I don't want to be commercial?"

"That's not what I said." She rolled her wrist, checked her watch, not even hiding it. "You can break the rules, but you have to know why you're breaking them. Otherwise, it just sounds—" She stopped, shook her head. "Never mind."

I was so desperate for the last word that I interrupted. "Sounds like a cry for help?"

Shiloh shrugged. "You said it."

I made a show of fixing my cuff, pulling the sleeve so tight it nearly cut off circulation. "It's not my fault the label wants three-minute pop when I'm giving them an exorcism."

"Is that what this is?" She tilted her head again, clinical. "Because it sounds like you're holding back."

I almost told her about the last year, about the insomnia and the noise in my head and the way every day felt like an audition for a role I'd already been cut from. Instead, I looked straight at her, past the clinical neatness, at the mole above her eyebrow that only showed up in fluorescent lighting.

I said, "You used to call my demos 'unhinged, but at least it's alive.' You get promoted and now you want everything safe?"

Her mouth twitched, half a smile or half a snarl, couldn't tell which. "I want it honest."

"That's what this is." My hands were fidgety now, but I held them under the table, out of her line of sight.

She sighed, the first sign of fatigue. "Bishop, if you want to make something nobody else can do, you have to risk it not working. You used to take more risks."

That landed harder than I'd admit. Blood pounded in my ears. I spun the ring on my finger one more time, then let it go. "Okay. I'll try harder."

"We can start over. If you want."

It took me three seconds too long to realize she meant the song.

My breath caught. Just a hitch, barely there, but I felt it. Start over. The words took hold and I didn't know what to do with them. Didn't know what to do with my hands. My face was probably doing something weird, too. "Yeah," I heard myself say, and it came out smaller.

Thinner. "Let's do that."

I watched her cue up a blank project, hands moving in a blur, and told myself it didn't matter how much of the old language she still remembered. I was here to make a song. Not to open a vein and bleed for her approval.

But my leg kept bouncing, and I couldn't stop it.

Shiloh killed the previous session with a single click, then started laying out a new blank—tempo grid first, then a dummy kit with zero personality. "Strip it?" she asked, not looking up.

"Strip it," I flexed my hands. "Start with a raw take."

She nodded, then set to work, muting all the reference layers until only a skeleton was left. Her hands on the console moved fast, deliberate, almost greedy. She cued up a new track, slid the fader up just enough to ghost the input.

From this angle, the blue vein at her wrist. The floral scent hung around her like static electricity. She leaned close and suddenly I was back in our last bad fight. Scorched coffee, tears neither of us admitted to. I inhaled, held it too long, let it go with a practiced yawn.

"Mic's patched," she said, already pulling up the reference sheet. "You remember the lyrics?"

I glared. "Better than you."

She finally looked up. Eyes soft, just for a second, then all business again. "Booth's hot. You want reverb or clean?"

"Clean. I'll do my own echo."

She almost smiled. "Sure." Her voice sounded like it belonged to someone else.

I walked to the booth. The booth had the old Neumann, the one with the dent in the mesh from a dropped stand in 2019. I set the headphones on. I tapped the glass.

Shiloh, back at the console, flicked the talkback. "Test when ready."

I closed my eyes, counted down from four, then rapped the first two bars, barely above a whisper. I sang it again, louder, then waited for feedback.

Shiloh's voice came through the phones: "Pitch is good. Try for more dynamic on the bridge. You're flattening out at the pre-chorus."

"Copy," I said.

We ran it four more times, Shiloh calling for adjustments through the talkback. By the fifth, my throat felt aggy.

On take six, I lost the lyric halfway through and filled the gap with a nonsense vowel, not even a word, just a moan at the back of my tongue. The sound vibrated through the headphones, a little ugly, too honest.

The talkback popped. This time, her voice was different—less cold, more awake. "Let's, uh. Keep that. Do the whole second verse with that energy."

I blinked. "You want it fucked-up?"

"I want it real." She paused. "That's what we always did best."

Shiloh turned back to the board before I could see her face properly. Hands already moving, pulling up a track, doing something—anything—that wasn't looking at me.

The words hit me like a needle to the vein. I swallowed, then started the verse again, pushing harder, letting the last syllable drag. I ad-libbed a line on the repeat, something I knew she'd recognize. A callback to the Harmony Heights sessions, when we'd make each other laugh in the booth and try to work it into the track so nobody else would notice.

After, I finished the run and just stood there, letting the air out in slow hisses. The headphones felt heavier than they should.

It used to be easy, when she was just a memory—ache dulled by distance, background noise I could tune out if I tried hard enough. But having her this close, sharing the same air, the same song—it was pressing on a bruise to see if it still hurt. Spoiler: it did. And I couldn't look at her without wanting to go back, just for a second, to before everything got so fucked-up between us.

Through the glass, Shiloh was stone still, one hand on the board, the other covering her mouth. She played the last take back, soloed my voice, then played it again, stopping at the ad-lib. She looped the section. On the fourth loop, her shoulders dropped—just a fraction, the tension releasing before she caught herself. Then she blinked, and the wall went back up. Face blank. Professional.

Finally, Shiloh pressed the intercom again. Her tone was softer, the mask back on but not as thick. "That's the take," she said. "You nailed it."

I pretended not to care. I took off the headphones, set them on the mic, and stepped out.

Shiloh didn't look at me. She was already splicing the take into the master track, fingers flying across the keys. "You want to comp another or leave it as is?"

I shrugged. "You tell me. Producer's choice."

"Let's not overthink it for once."

"Copy that." I leaned against the side wall, letting my arms hang loose, trying to shake off the aftertaste of being seen.

The room was so quiet, my pulse thumped in my own ears. I watched her play the section back, eyes flicking to the timeline, then back to the screen. She soloed the track, leaned in close, and closed her eyes for a half second as the ad-lib rolled through.

We spent the next two hours fighting over a drop.

Not with screaming—nothing so messy, nothing so honest. Just: loop, listen, argue, loop again. Shiloh's style was to nudge the arrangement toward "maturity," which in practice meant sandpapering off everything that might offend a playlist algorithm. I wanted the drop to hit early, to shock the blood awake and make it impossible to ignore. She wanted a slow burn, a build, a payoff that didn't show up until minute three.

"It's punchier if we cut straight from the break to the chorus," I said, leaning over her shoulder to stab at the screen. "This, right here. The anticipation's already there—no reason to string it out."

She didn't look up from the DAW. "But if you tease it out, the release means more. People remember the back half, not the first impact."

"People are cowards," I muttered, but not quiet enough.

She smiled with half of her mouth. "You don't have to call the audience names to make your point."

"I'm not talking about the audience."

She let it pass. "Fine. Let's try your way."

I watched her hands as she copied the section, slicing the grid with clinical neatness, then dragging the drop forward. She soloed the transition, letting it play back. The shift was abrupt, the way I wanted it. My voice crashed in over the synth, and for a second I felt the old rush—like a punch to the chest, like jumping off a roof and landing on your feet.

"There," I said. "See?"

She looped it three more times, volume low. Her eyes narrowed, not in anger, just in calculation.

"I get the energy. But you lose the runway. It's all tension, no payoff."

"Not every story has to resolve," I shot back. "Some things are better unresolved."

She didn't answer, just looped the section again, this time with the harmonies up and the drums low. The ad-lib I'd buried in the last take poked through, a tiny gasp in the middle of the phrase. It sounded raw, maybe a little ugly. I waited for her to cut it, to erase the evidence.

But she left it in.

The last twenty minutes were a slow fade. We ran the final version twice, then went through the checklist: stems exported, levels checked, a rough mix bounced for the label. I packed up my things—spiral notebook, battered water bottle, jacket. I did it slow, on purpose, in case she wanted to say something else.

She didn't.

At the door, I looked back. Shiloh was hunched at the console, head-phones pulled half-on, looping the same four bars of my vocal. I watched her, just for a second, as she soloed the ad-lib again, letting it echo in the silence.

But I didn't ask. I just watched her, still as a photograph, the pale blue light from the monitor painting shadows across her cheekbones. For once, she didn't look back.

I left. The door shut behind me with a sound too soft to be final.

I sat in my car for a solid ten minutes before even touching the ignition. Hands on the wheel, music off, with the warmth of the leather seeping into my palms. I stared through the windshield at nothing but shadows of street furniture and cigarette butts.

You'd think making music would be catharsis, right? Sometimes it was. Tonight, it was just another way to rip myself open and then staple-gun the skin back down. I told myself the tension was about the track, about the label's expectations, about how nothing ever felt finished. I didn't think about the way Shiloh looped my voice like she was searching for a pulse, or the fact that the part of me that hated her most at the moment was also the part that wanted her to never stop listening.

Last time with the doc crew all up in the control room, I just—handled it. Didn't even think. Saw Shiloh's shoulders climbing toward her ears, that jaw clench she does when there's too many bodies breathing her air, and I was already moving. Started yapping about mic placement, about Jinx's whole setup, led them out like the Pied Piper of annoying film dudes. Used to do the same thing at Harmony Heights, too. Kick people out when she needed the room quiet enough to think. Four years, and my body still knew the drill. Still wanted to protect her space. Couldn't do that shit with anyone else, either. Just her.

My head fell against the steering wheel, eyes shut, counting my heartbeat in the darkness.

The thing about being this down bad for someone? It made you do the dumbest shit just to stop feeling it for five seconds. At least I could get Skye's titties in my face while doing it.

I texted Skye.

> *u up or are u having an Emotion again*

The reply came back in seven seconds.

> *I never have emotions after midnight, you know this*

I typed:

> *u a damn lie*

She replied:

> *you coming over or clowning? pick one.*

I didn't answer. I just locked the phone, started the engine, and let the car crawl down the street.

Her apartment was on the north side, above a Korean BBQ that smelled like burned sugar and smoke. The entry code was the same as always, 0826, the day she got her first solo radio placement. I punched it in with the same way I used to play scales.

Skye answered the door in an oversized tee, no makeup, hair a curtain over one eye. She looked at me, took in the jacket, the kicks, the way I kept my hands shoved in the pockets. She grinned, toothy and sharp.

"Nice of you to remember I exist," she said.

I stepped inside, let the door close behind me. Kicked off my sneakers at the door. The apartment was small but stacked—a wall of records, couch that doubled as a graveyard for lost socks, kitchen counter littered with half-finished song journals. The only light was from a pink lava lamp and the neon from the barbecue sign outside. No music played, which was unusual; Skye usually had something blasting, even if it was just a looped drum machine.

She flopped onto the couch, feet up, then patted the cushion next to her. "So. How'd it go?"

I rolled my eyes, sat beside her, close but not touching. "As well as you'd expect."

She laughed, a short bark. "So world war three but with more passive aggression."

"More like, cold war with a lot of facial tics."

She grinned, stretching her arms behind her head. "You two always were predictable."

I shrugged. "Thought you were on my side."

She reached for the vape pen on the coffee table, took a long drag, then blew the cloud at the ceiling. "I'm on the side of drama. Yours is always top-tier."

My head fell back against the sofa, staring up at the shadow-laced ceiling. "You ever think maybe I should just quit? Walk out, let the label implode, get a job at Trader Joe's or something?"

Skye laughed again, but it was softer this time. "Nah. You'd get fired for hijacking the PA system."

I wanted to argue, but she wasn't wrong. I probably would hack the intercom just to play bootleg mixtapes on shift.

She turned, eyes on me, the weird light making her irises look almost gold. "You want to talk about it?"

I shook my head. "Nope."

She didn't push it. She never did.

Instead, she slid closer, her thigh pressed against mine. The air in the apartment felt charged, but not in a way that hurt. It was like a blackout—everything turned off, nothing left to do but find warmth in the dark.

Skye leaned in, not for a kiss (that's rule one: no kissing, no matter how bad you want it), but just enough to rest her forehead against mine. She smelled like dragonfruit and the fabric softener she never rinsed off all the way. Her hand found my wrist, thumb tracing the veins there, soft and steady.

That was rule two: if someone catches feelings, game over, no exceptions. Rule three: no sleeping over. Rule four: keep it clean, get tested, don't be an idiot. We were good at rules. We had to be.

"You're a mess," she said, almost affectionate.

"Says the queen of mess," I shot back, but my voice was hoarse.

"That's Ms. Bella to you." She squeezed my wrist, then pulled me toward the bedroom. I let myself be led, because that was the deal—she never made it weird, never asked for more than I could give.

We didn't talk. We didn't need to. The rest was hands and teeth, clothes dragged up and over, the soft punch of skin on skin. Not gentle but never mean. We fucked like two people who had nowhere else to be and nothing left to lose.

After, I lay there on her mattress, sweat cooling in the blue glow from the sign outside. Skye's breath was slow and even, her arm folded over her stomach. I zoned out, staring at the cracked plaster on the ceiling and tried to feel something more than the static in my head. The emptiness gnawed at me—so I reached for her again, hand slipping over her hip, hoping maybe another round would burn through the numbness. Skye didn't say anything, just shifted a little, making room, letting me try.

Somewhere between the second round and the finish line, Skye did something she'd never done before. She slipped her hand behind my neck, slow and deliberate, and cradled my skull like it was fragile, like I was something breakable.

It wasn't rough. It wasn't even gentle. It was—something else. Like she was asking me to stay, right there, in that moment.

Every muscle in me went rigid. My eyes snapped open. I waited for the other shoe to drop, for the joke or the bite or the pointed dig, but it never came. Instead, Skye's hand slid up, cupping my face, thumb tracing the line of my jaw, stroking slow at my hairline. She studied me for a heartbeat, then tipped my chin up.

"Lay back," I said, rough under my breath. Skye didn't argue as I pushed her legs all the way back. She shifted beneath me, melting into the mattress, and I climbed over her, sliding back inside, the heat of her swallowing me whole.

We moved together, her anklet dangling over my shoulder. When she reached up, trying to touch my face again, I caught her wrists and pinned them above her head, fingers laced tight.

The look she gave me, half challenge, half surrender, made my stomach drop. I fucked her slow, steady, held the rhythm even when I wanted to wreck it. She tensed under me. Tremor starting at her core and rippling out. Breathing ragged. Body shuddering as she came, hard. A name that wasn't mine slipping out like something she'd been choking on.

I heard it. Pretended I didn't.

Fucking *Cam*. Ruined a good nut, yet again.

All I could do was hold on, heart pounding so loud it drowned out everything else—heat and chills colliding under my skin, wanting too much and not enough, all at once. I released my grip on her wrists.

I forced myself to close my eyes again. Her hips kept moving, the tempo slowing, less frenetic now, more measured, like we were both waiting for a sign that never showed. When it was over, we just lay there—bodies touching but hearts not even in the same room. My own body still tight, unsatisfied, nerves singing like feedback. The harness was starting to get on my nerves, now. I unbuckled myself.

Skye glanced over her shoulder, clocked my clenched jaw, and snorted softly. "You're always too proud to ask when you need something, Bishop." Before I could answer, her hand slid down, finding me with ease. "Don't say I never do anything for you," she muttered, but there was no real heat behind it.

She touched me until I came, sharp and fast, nothing romantic about it. Just a release valve hissing open. After, Skye rolled onto her side, back to me, one arm draped across her own chest like she was protecting something.

It didn't feel like closeness. Just two people, keeping each other from drowning, one small favor at a time.

Cam's Very Unhelpful Update

Shiloh

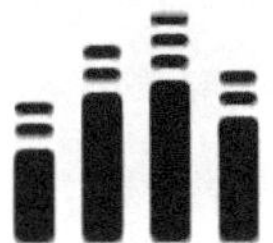

Glass walls, black marble countertops, every inch screaming "somebody's making more and it's not you." The venue tonight—Magma, near the river—looked like a tech billionaire's panic room. Everything shiny, cold, and engineered to make people feel important even when they were just killing time between projects.

I kept to the edge. Too much light in the center, too many people trying to clock who was talking to who. My corner: bar-height table against the window, view of the whole circus but close enough to the exit that I could make a clean break if needed. Standard uniform—black blazer, pressed shirt, slacks that looked like they were tailored even though I'd hemmed them myself. Watch cleaned yesterday. Chelsea at the label said "casual but elevated" so I left the jewelry in the drawer and stuck with black-on-black. No distractions.

Drink in hand. Bourbon, neat. I let the glass sweat condensation onto my fingers but didn't take more than a mouthful every ten minutes. This was for show, not for pleasure. I wanted a clear head.

Conference badges stacked by the door, but nobody wore them. You knew most faces already—producers, A&R, managers in monochrome suits, a handful of songwriters playing dress-up. The rest hovered at the periphery, hoping proximity would turn into access. I traded "hey, good to see you," "let's circle back," "congrats on the project" on repeat for the first half hour. After that, people mostly left me alone.

The venue ran on light strips—every wall cycling deep blue to gold. The drinks tasted expensive, but every sip just made my mouth drier. The air: perfume, sweat, and that synthetic lemon from the cleaning crew.

Midway through my first drink, Cam Wolfe came over.

She didn't do the slow approach. Just appeared, steady and weightless, wearing an open button-down and floral pants. The shirt showed off her neck tattoo in a way that made it hard not to look. Even dressed just this side of androgynous, Cam was almost too pretty to look at—like the lines of her face refused to stay understated. Always had been. She gave me a real smile, no teeth, just soft at the edges, like she'd been saving it.

"Ellis," she said. Not a question.

I gave her a fist bump. "Wolfe."

We posted up at the bar, side by side. Our reflections in the counter: her jaw, sharp as always. Mine, a little tired, maybe, but holding the line.

She reached for a gin and tonic, ice clattering, and leaned in so her words wouldn't carry. "Tell me you're not here for these people."

I snorted. "I'm here so the label can say I showed my face."

She nodded, satisfied. "That's what I figured. You never did go for the open bar."

I shrugged. "Never saw the appeal. Free doesn't mean good."

She took a sip, wiped a drop from her lower lip. "Still, they're pouring better than last year. Remember that launch at the Riverside? I thought the vodka was going to take the paint off my teeth."

"I do remember. You traded your drink for my Pellegrino and acted like you were doing me a favor."

She grinned, slow and genuine. "What can I say? I'm a giver."

This was Cam at her best. No bullshit, no posturing. Just say what you mean, mean what you say.

She set her glass down, body turned so we were open but private. "I wanted to say—I listened to V2 last night, and hate that we didn't get to go further than that. You're a magician. I don't know how you made those adlibs blend. It was a car crash before you got in there."

I resisted the urge to look away. Praise always sounded like a trick, even from Cam. But her eyes were direct. No games.

"You made it easy," I said, voice low. "Your vocal's got this—grain at the edges. Like it wants to break but never does."

"That's just dehydration and inherited trauma." She smiled again, but there was an old ache underneath. "Seriously, though. I know you're busy right now, but I want to work with you on the EP. I can tell you're not going to bullshit me."

Cam had been chewed up by this business more than once, left standing anyway. Still led with kindness. Still tried to build something that would last longer than a Fizzr cycle.

I didn't say "thank you." Just let the moment settle.

"That's what's up. I'm in," I said, simple.

The background buzz was a comfort. Cam didn't rush, didn't talk to fill silence. We'd always had that—could sit through ten seconds of nothing and not get nervous. It was the opposite of Bishop, who would set drums on fire before letting dead air win.

I rolled the glass against my palm. "How's legal handling the fallout with the leak?"

She made a neck-cutting gesture. "I mean, you didn't hear this from me, but they're out for blood. Forensics is on it. Whoever did it, they're going to make things expensive for them"

"Ouch."

For a half-minute, I could pretend the rest of the world didn't exist. It was just two people who knew the cost of getting this far and could laugh about it anyway.

I liked that. I liked her.

Across the room, I caught movement in my periphery. Bishop had arrived. The energy shifted before I even turned my head. I heard the boots: step, drag, slide, all attitude. When I glanced over, she was already cutting through the crowd in a cropped lemon-lime jacket and baggy jeans, sunglasses indoors, because fuck you.

She hit her marks perfectly. Leaned into the A&R exec.'s space, made him show all his teeth. Touched the inside of a songwriter's fore-arm—intimate as a secret handshake. Each interaction a controlled detonation, then she'd move on before anyone could ask for more.

I'd seen her sit cross-legged on a basement couch in PJs, controller in hand, barely saying a word except to narrate her own victories in a ter-rible announcer voice. "And Bishop with the FLAWLESS execution! The crowd goes wild!" She'd bump my shoulder every time she won, grinning like an idiot. This performance wasn't Evienne. It was the cost of being Bishop.

I turned back to Cam.

Laughter got sharper, more pronounced. Closer. The DJ dropped the volume, and in the gap you could hear Bishop's laugh slice the air. I didn't even have to turn—knew she'd pull up soon as she clocked me with Cam.

I tried to brace for it. Didn't help.

She landed next to me, all heat and angles, her scent a chemical slap after Cam's herbal. Bishop owned three feet of air everywhere she stood. She didn't wait for a gap—just shoved herself into the flow.

"Look at y'all," she said, big grin, sunglasses still on. "Ellis and Wolfe, together again? This is industry black magic. Somebody take a picture."

Cam didn't react, just lifted her chin in greeting. "Hey, Bishop."

Bishop leaned her elbow on the bar, so close I saw where the jacket lining had started to fray. She looked at my drink, snorted. "Damn, Shiloh, you out here sipping like you're at a chess tournament. Gonna need you to up the tempo."

"Some of us like to taste our poison," I said, refusing the bait.

Bishop laughed, too loud for the space. "Not me. I'm full-commit or nothing." She flagged the bartender with a finger, ordered "whatever looks like liquid sunshine, extra weird, no garnish." Didn't clarify. Didn't need to.

She pivoted to Cam. "You still riding high off that last single? I heard the remix but damn—didn't realize you were trying to start street fights on Spotify."

Cam's mouth curled, slow. "I figure if I can't make 'em mad, I'm not working hard enough."

"That's why we love you." Bishop nudged my arm, like I was supposed to join in. "Don't we love her, Shiloh?"

I set my glass down, deliberate. "Cam brings heat, no doubt."

This should've been fun. Instead, Bishop was pushing. Dial cranked past the number.

She started doing her thing—insider gossip, throwing out names, "Y'all heard about the video shoot that got shut down eastside?" or "Did you see who got dropped from their pub deal last week?" She had a story for every scenario, all with herself at the center. She wanted to be the sun.

Cam played along, but cool. No over-laughing, no wide eyes. Just chill, nodding, letting Bishop do the heavy lifting.

I watched the games stack up: Bishop making jokes. She talked over Cam, recast any comment as a punchline, even steered the conversation to a time "three A&Rs tried to poach me at a Label Showcase and failed, 'cause my people are loyal, right Shiloh?" She shot me a look with it, clearly was fishing for a response.

I didn't bite.

Then Bishop dropped the first bomb.

She lowered her voice, conspiratorial. "By the way—heard about that leak. That's fucking brutal." She glanced around the room, then back at Cam. "You're brave as hell showing up here, though. What if Romi walks in?"

Cam flinched, but she hid it well. "Then she walks in."

"Yeah, but—" Bishop gestured vaguely. "After that unfinished track hit the internet? Wild timing."

"It is what it is." Cam's voice was flat, bored even.

Bishop pressed, couldn't help herself. "Any idea who—"

"Nope." Cam cut her off clean. "And I'm not looking."

The tone was pure troll, fishing for a reaction. But Cam didn't give her one.

Cam had a way of letting the conversation pass right through her. Like wind through an open window. She wasn't threatened. She didn't even seem annoyed. The more Bishop amped up, the less Cam gave back.

Then Cam did the thing: looked at Bishop, not away, but right through. "Tell Skye I said what's up."

She waited just long enough to let it land, then turned and left without looking back. Casual, easy. Like she'd just shut down a heckler and moved on to dessert.

Made sense that things would be awkward with Skye's name out there. Cam and Skye's breakup had been public enough—screaming match that made the press, subtweets, the whole mess.

I clocked the expression on Bishop's face but didn't touch it yet.

For a minute, the pulse of the party faded out. Light, color, chatter—it all went muffled, like someone had dropped a comforter over the room. Bishop shifted her weight, one foot bracing against the bar rail. Her mouth tried to twist up in a smile that landed dead on arrival.

She made a weird noise between a cough and a laugh. "Damn, Cam's been taking savage lessons. Didn't know she and Skye even talked. Small fuckin' world, right?" She rolled her eyes, but the performance was flat. The air around her shook; her fingers thrummed a nervous code against the condensation of her glass.

She didn't look at me.

I tracked every tell, the way I tracked the phase noise in a dirty vocal stem. Her right hand was flexing, ring digging awkward against her skin. She laughed again, smaller, and dropped her chin so the shades hid most of her face.

It hit me, suddenly, why Bishop might've gotten caught up with her. Skye didn't have tells; she *was* the tell. I remembered that slow-motion video from last year, the one that went viral: Skye in a catsuit, tossing her hair and glancing back over her shoulder, ass wobbling just enough to break the algorithm. Even I'd watched it more than once, trying to figure out what made it look so easy. I got it. I understood why people made dummies of themselves over her. Why Bishop might, too.

The pieces assembled themselves in my head with the certainty of a mix coming into focus. The room got warmer. Or I did. The production meeting. Bishop's reaction when I suggested Skye Bella for vocals—too fast, too defensive. "Not Skye." No explanation, just immediate shutdown. I'd filed it away as Bishop being difficult, controlling the session roster. But Cam just assumed Bishop had direct access to Skye. Assumed Bishop would be the one delivering messages.

And Bishop's tells right now—the nervous energy, the deflection, the refusal to make eye contact—looked exactly like they did in the booth when she was trying to hide something real behind the performance.

I didn't let her pivot.

No volume, no venom. I stepped in closer. Behind the sunglasses, her expression shifted, went soft and focused at once. I'd seen it before. Right before she kissed me for only the second time ever, years ago, both of us pretending we were just working.

I said, "Who you fuck isn't my business anymore. But that was kinda messy. I don't do messy."

She laughed, but it sounded like air leaking from a tire. "You're the one leaning in and looking at me like that, but I'm the messy one? Okay."

I didn't move. Didn't blink.

"Yeah," she said, voice dropping lower. "You don't do messy. Got it. So, what's this?" She gestured between us—the six inches of charged air, the way I hadn't stepped back yet. "Because from where I'm standing, you just got in my space to tell me you don't care who I'm sleeping with. Which sounds like you care."

My jaw tightened.

"Okay, first of all—I'm single, so like, legally I can do whatever the fuck I want, right?" Bishop's words came fast, defensive. "And I didn't bring Skye into this, Cam did, because apparently she's on some reality TV villain timing tonight, so if you wanna be mad at someone, be mad at her—"

She stopped. Watched my face.

"But you're not." Her voice changed. Quieter. "You're not mad at her. You're mad at *me*."

My pulse jumped.

She tilted her head, and something shifted in her expression—sharper now, less performative.

"So pick one." She wasn't joking anymore. Wasn't deflecting. Just standing there, looking at me like she was daring me to walk away. "Either it's none of your business and you walk away. Or it is your business—"

Her jaw worked, like she was forcing the words out.

"And we talk about why you're still looking at me like that." Her eyes dropped to my mouth. She flinched, stepped back.

The room felt smaller. Loud. My heart was louder and wildly inconvenient. I needed to leave.

"I'm going to get another drink," I said.

Her shoulders sagged.

I stepped back, turned, walked. Steady pace, shoulders square. Across the room, straight line to the bar.

I wasn't jealous, especially not over someone who left *me*. You only ever got to show me once you don't want me. I'm out.

Jealousy would mean I cared who Bishop was sleeping with. I didn't. This was about professional boundaries. About not letting her personal mess bleed into my work. That's all.

The lean in was proximity. The room was loud. I needed her to hear me.

At the bar, I ordered water. Took the glass. Didn't drink.

Behind me, somewhere in the crowd, Bishop was probably back to performing. Good. That's what we both did best—move on, stay professional.

I was fine.

Here's Where You Start Feeling Personally Attacked

Bishop

I STOOD IN THE hallway of my apartment, staring at the cologne bottle on the dresser.

Thick glass. Heavy enough to knock someone out if you swung it hard enough. I'd already changed three times. Settled on the band tee, black jeans still stiff from being new, the jacket that made my arms look bigger. Keys in hand. Bag packed. Ready to leave.

Except I kept staring at that bottle.

"Don't do it, fam," I muttered to myself.

It was the same scent I'd worn back then. The same one Shiloh always noticed, even when she pretended not to. She'd never said anything direct—that wasn't her style—but I'd catch her leaning in closer when we worked, or the way her jaw would tighten when I'd show up to the studio smelling like I'd just rolled out of someone else's bed (which, to be fair, I usually had). The time she straight up sniffed my neck, we made out in the equipment room until my hands were in her jeans.

I picked up the bottle. Put it down. Picked it up again.

This was stupid. Pathetic, even. What was I trying to do? Trigger some Pavlovian response? Make her remember something she'd probably worked very hard to forget?

I sprayed it twice on my throat, anyway.

I grabbed the messenger bag off the kitchen table, the one still crammed with old lyric sheets and crumpled grocery receipts. Shoved the laptop inside, then zipped it up. Left the apartment a disaster. Slammed the door, then walked back to make sure I'd actually locked it.

On the drive to the studio, I turned the radio to full blast and let it play whatever came up: indie pop, old Dev Royale, a jingle for a law firm with an easy-to-remember number. My fingers drummed out a rhythm on the steering wheel, tight and unsteady.

I made every green light without trying. At every stop, I checked my phone—no new emails, no messages from Shiloh.

At the last intersection before the studio, I caught myself in the rearview. My mouth was pressed firm. I stuck my tongue out at my own face, then laughed. It came out thin and dry.

The cologne felt too obvious now. Too loud. Like showing up with a sign that said "remember when you used to want me?" I wished I'd popped a gummy to keep myself from being so wound up. It's just Shiloh.

Except the last time I saw her, she couldn't get away from me fast enough. The memory of it made me want to crawl right out of my skin.

Pulled up to the curb. Killed the engine.

I sat there for a second, hand on the ignition, toying with the idea of turning the car around.

One more breath, then I opened the door. The night air was colder than I expected.

Down the stairs. Past the keypad. Down the hall.

At the end of it, Shiloh's studio door was already open, the faint thrum of our last mix pulsing through the gap.

I didn't knock. Just went in.

The mix hit before I even cleared the threshold—bass running warm through the floor, kick like a pulse you could almost dance to if your life depended on it. The whole room was shot in indigo from the neon accent lights, so everything looked hyper-real and a little dangerous. Shiloh was at the console, back straight, hands on the dials. She didn't look up.

I lingered in the doorway for a second, waiting for the usual "hey" or at least a glance. Nothing. She was already mid-session, surgical. The left monitor was soloed, my voice doubling back at me from a half-finished verse. I heard every flaw. I wondered if she did too.

She spoke, not turning. "The label wants the bridge done first. They're pushing for a rough tonight, even if it's just scratch vocals. If we get that, the rest is cleanup."

No "hi." No joke about my outfit. She'd skipped right to the work like we'd never skipped a beat.

I edged into the room, set my bag by the wall, and looked for a chair that didn't make me look like I was hiding. There wasn't one, so I just leaned against the old upright piano near the sound baffles.

"Good to see you too, Ellis," I said, voice dry as the snack bar in the lobby. "You ever take a day off from the militarized production schedule?"

Her head tilted an inch, a concession, but she didn't look over. "You want this finished or not?"

I shrugged, pretending it didn't sting. "I mean, that's what they pay you for, right?"

Now she did look. The studio lights splashed across her glasses, so I couldn't read her expression. "I don't get paid enough to babysit your anxiety."

I could've said it. Could've thrown it right back to her. Yeah, how's it feel, working for a check instead of a legacy? But watching her jaw tighten, I realized she already knew. She was living it.

If it was supposed to hurt, I didn't let it. "No one does," I said, and managed a smile. It didn't land.

Shiloh clicked the track to a stop. Silence crashed in, making my skin crawl.

She exhaled, audible. "Look, the creative team's sending their notes in an hour. If we don't have something by then, they'll just keep escalating."

"Classic," I said. "Nothing says 'creative freedom' like corporate panic."

No answer. She switched windows on the monitor, fingers moving in clean, precise keystrokes. Every gesture telegraphed how little room there was for me in the process.

I drifted closer, just to feel something. "So, what's the plan? You want to loop the bridge until I hate myself, or do you want to start on the last verse?"

Shiloh inhaled sharply through her nose. Quick, involuntary, then held it. Her fingers froze on the keyboard for half a second before resuming their crawl. "I'm already looping it."

The track started again, this time with the vocal muted. Her eyes ticked between the screen and the waveform, tuning out my presence as if I were another plug-in to route and automate.

I moved closer to the mixing board. The keys were cold against my palms. Vaguely, I thought about making another joke—something about how the old days at Harmony Heights were more fun, or how I missed when we used to get high before sessions—but the room felt like it would swallow the words whole.

I watched Shiloh's hands, the way she cued up the next section, the way she refused to let any silence hang. She was building a sonic barricade, one fader at a time.

She finally spoke, voice stripped of affect, "We should focus on the bridge section first."

"Whatever you want," I said, and meant it.

She cued the playback. The hook ran, then the empty eight bars—my cue to fill in, to make it bleed. I watched the screen, watched the seconds tick down, the little digital clock echoing my own heartbeat. I almost laughed at myself.

"Can you solo it?" I asked. "Just the drums?"

She did, efficient. "You want the click, or just the groove?"

"Both," I said. "I like to suffer."

A flicker at the corner of her mouth, gone before it fully formed.

I stared at the monitor. "You know, the last time we did this, you wouldn't let me touch a mic until we'd eaten, like, two pizzas, and bitched about everyone we hated in the program. Now it's all business."

She didn't look up. "People change."

I hesitated, pulse stuttering, then fished for something I probably didn't want the real answer to. "What about me? Am I the exception?"

Shiloh's fingers paused on the console, but she didn't turn. "No one's the exception forever, Bishop."

The room felt smaller, the air heavier. I let the drums run, feeling the tempo through the soles of my shoes.

In the silence between takes, I risked a glance at her face. She looked tired, but in a way that was like she didn't know how else to be.

She'd been looping the same eight bars for fifteen minutes, tweaking the high-end until the hi-hats sounded like they were recorded in a tin can. Every few minutes, she'd undo the change, then redo it, then undo it again.

I watched her hover over the EQ, fingers twitching on the mouse.

"That sounds worse," I finally said.

"It's not mixed yet."

"No, I mean worse than it did five minutes ago. And ten minutes ago. And—"

"I heard you."

She cut the highs even more. Now it sounded like we were underwater.

I bit my tongue. This was the Shiloh who'd keep us here until sunrise, destroying perfectly good takes because she couldn't sit still with whatever she was actually feeling. I'd seen her scrap entire sessions this way—not because the work was bad, but because she needed to control something.

I cleared my throat. "You want me in the booth?"

She stopped. Looked at me like I'd suggested we set the studio on fire.

"For what?"

"The bridge. You said it needed vocals."

"I said it might need vocals. I haven't decided yet."

"Okay, well while you're deciding, I could—"

"I need to finish this first."

She went back to the EQ. Boosted the same frequency she'd just cut.

I stood up. "Shiloh."

"What."

"You're making it worse."

She frowned. "I'm working."

"No, you're avoiding. I know what that looks like."

She didn't answer. Just soloed the drums and started cutting frequencies that didn't need cutting.

I walked to the booth door, opened it. "I'm getting in the booth. You can use me or not, but at least it'll give you something else to focus on besides destroying that snare."

She looked at me then. Her eyes were tired, angry, something else underneath I couldn't name.

"Fine," she said finally. "When you're ready."

I stood, rolled my shoulders, tried to shake off the feeling that I was already failing. At the door to the booth, I turned. "You sure you don't want to make it weird first?"

It used to mean a million things. Sharing a blunt, talking shit, sometimes just blowing off steam the way only we could, even if it meant hands wandering where they shouldn't. Now it just sounded like a joke with no one on the other end.

This time, she didn't answer at all. Just clicked the track back to zero and waited.

I stepped into the booth, closed the door. The air inside was thicker, the glass a perfect barrier. Shiloh watched through the window, posture locked in.

I put on the headphones. My hands probably gripped them too hard.

The talkback clicked on, her voice clean and precise: "Mic's hot. Whenever."

I stared straight ahead, willing my heart to slow down.

She played the track, and I let the bridge breathe, let it fill me up.

Even with the glass between us, the tension was thick as grits. It was in the way she never looked up. It was in the way the air refused to move.

I cued up.

The first take was technically fine. At least, I thought it was. But before I even finished the last note, Shiloh's voice came through the talkback: "Again."

No explanation. No feedback.

I ran it again. Got through the whole thing this time, felt pretty good about it actually, and—

"Again."

"What was wrong with that one?"

"Just run it again."

Third take. I adjusted my approach, went softer on the opening, pushed harder on the resolve. Finished strong.

Silence.

"The timing's off."

"Where?"

"All of it."

I pressed my hand against the glass. "*Shiloh.* What do you actually want?"

"I want you to sing it right."

"I am singing it right. You're just not hearing it because you're pissed at me!"

Her shoulders went up. For a second I thought she might cut the talkback, leave me in here to suffocate on my own voice.

Instead: "One more. From the top."

I wanted to argue. Wanted to push back, make her talk to me like a person instead of like I was just another track she could loop until it stopped bothering her.

But it was all up in her face—the set of her shoulders, the way she kept adjusting levels that didn't need adjusting. She wouldn't look at me through the glass, and I didn't know what to do with that. It tied my stomach up in tight knots.

So I sang it again. And again. And again.

We did seven in total. I could almost feel the bruise rising at the base of my throat, that special, bitter ache you only get from singing at the edge of your own destruction. I hated it. I loved it.

After the seventh, she gave me a pause long enough to hope for feedback, then just said, "Got it."

I waited for more, but the red light over the door clicked off.

I came out of the booth, headphones dangling from my neck, and stood there, hoping she'd say something. She didn't. Just dragged the files into the session, comped the takes, fingers moving fast on the keyboard, all business.

She soloed the new bridge, listened once, then hard-panned the vocals left. "This needs layering. Otherwise, it's thin." She flagged the edit and went right to slicing the next track.

I spoke up, half joke, half plea. She was not about to strong-arm her way into deleting one of my stems again. "You know you're legally not allowed to ignore my input, right? The contract says 'creative collaboration.' It's in the fine print."

"I'm not ignoring you. I'm just working."

"Feels like the same thing."

She didn't even look at me. "It's not."

Flat. Final. Like slamming a door in my face.

I leaned against the desk, arms crossed. "Can we try the second verse with less comp? Let it raw for a change?"

Shiloh paused, mouse hovering. Then clicked, like she'd decided to humor a child. "Sure."

She played it back. Every flaw was right there—breaths, a scrape on the *s*, a little stutter at the line about 'sharpened knives and paper crowns.' It sounded exposed, too naked.

But it was honest.

I waited for her to admit it. She didn't.

I tried again. "This is better, right? You said you wanted it honest."

She shrugged, not unkind, but final. "It's fine."

I tried to catch her eye. "If you wanted a perfect track, maybe you should've worked with Cam."

This got a reaction, finally. "Cam would've eaten the microphone."

"Maybe that's what the people want," I shot back. Even if it's mid. Kept that part to myself, because hearing her defend Cam right now might make me crash the entire fuck out.

Shiloh snorted, the smallest hint of humor, then killed it with a single button press.

Then, she layered in my voice, punched in harmonies I didn't remember recording. I watched her rebuild me, one decibel at a time.

I let the track play out, then said, "You remember when we used to do this at two in the morning, and you'd say 'let's wreck it, see what happens'?"

The words were out before I could stop them. Immediate regret—that was *our* thing, the reckless part of us that only existed together. I didn't know if I still got to reference it.

She nodded, but the memory wasn't sweet. "We were kids. There was nothing to lose."

"There's always something to lose," I said. "You just get better at hiding it."

She didn't reply, just busied herself with a different window.

I circled the room, restless, fingers drumming the back of the chair. Started to reach out—old instinct, my hand halfway to her shoulder before I caught myself. Shoved it in my pocket instead. I thought about Skye, about the way she'd held me before, about how none of it felt like comfort.

I stopped behind Shiloh, close enough to feel the heat coming off her back but careful not to touch. Four years ago, I would've just touched her. Would've leaned against her chair, played with her hair, made her laugh until she forgot to be careful with me.

Now, I stood there like a stranger, measuring distance. Shiloh had been doing this thing all session. Saying something sharp, then clamping down on whatever wanted to follow. Her jaw kept working, shoulders tight, as if she was physically holding words back. I could see the shape of what she wasn't saying in every rigid line of her body.

"You want to talk about it?"

She didn't even turn, but her back stiffened. "Talk about what?"

"You know what."

Now she spun the chair, slow and deliberate, so we were face-to-face. Her eyes were stone but not mean. Just tired. Long lashes fluttered open, closed, as she tried to keep her composure. It hit me, sudden as a slammed door—she looked older when she was pissed at me. Not old, but older, as if the years I'd chipped away at were finally showing.

"What exactly do you want from me, Bishop?"

The directness almost floored me. I scrambled for a joke, found none. Didn't think being just as direct would be helpful.

I said, "I just want this to not suck."

She held my gaze, searching for a lie. "Me too."

The silence stretched until it hurt.

Then, out of nowhere, I said it, "Okay, this is fucking awkward."

She didn't deflect. "Yeah. It is."

"We used to be better at this."

She looked at the board, at me, back to the board. "Maybe. Or maybe we just didn't notice."

I pressed, because I couldn't fucking hold this anymore: "Is it about Skye?"

"Do *not* flatter yourself." She scoffed and finally turned away. "Whatever's going on between you and Skye has nothing to do with me."

Shiloh locked back onto the screen, jaw tight, muscles braced like she was holding back a flood.

I knew that look. The way her shoulders set, the controlled breathing, the laser focus on the screen like if she stared hard enough the rest of the world would disappear. She was furious—not the kind that explodes, the kind that goes underground and eats you alive from the inside.

"Shiloh—"

"We should finish the track."

"Just say it." My voice came out rougher than I meant. "Just fucking say what you're actually feeling instead of doing this—" I gestured at her, at the screen, at the distance she was maintaining. "—whatever this is."

Her hands stilled on the console. For a second, I thought she might actually do it. Thought she might turn around and let me have it.

Instead, she said, quiet and lethal, "I'm working."

I stepped back, hands up. Surrender. "Fine. Let's just finish the track."

She didn't answer. She didn't have to.

We worked in silence for the next hour, trading files, marking edits, never touching. I watched her rebuild me, over and over, until what came out of the speakers was nothing like what I'd put in. I let her. I let it happen.

When it was over, the room felt emptier than when I'd arrived.

"You're okay with pretending this is fine?"

She finally spun the chair, faced me dead-on. "Nobody's pretending, Bishop. I just don't have the luxury of falling apart every time shit gets weird."

I wanted to argue, to tell her she was wrong, that she was just as much a mess as me, maybe more. But her face was stone—tired, yes, but resolved.

"Whatever you say, Shi."

She stood up, slow. Crossed the room, close enough that I saw the veins at her forearms, the half-healed cuts from a run-in with a broken cable.

"You think you're the only one who feels this? You think I wanted to end up here?"

I swallowed hard. "You never wanted anything enough to fight for it."

She flinched, barely, then shook her head. "That's not true. I just learned to fight smarter."

"Smarter." My voice cracked. "You mean safer. Behind your glass, your gear, your—you never had to risk everything."

"No." She cut me off, voice flat. "I just risked you."

The air went dead between us.

"So yeah, Evienne. I cared." Her voice cracked. "I cared so much I made myself *sick*. And when you walked away—no warning, no conversation, just *gone*—I had to teach myself how to be a person who didn't need you just to fucking *breathe*."

She stepped closer. Her fists were balled up.

"Don't tell me I didn't want it enough." The words came out jagged. "You have no idea what it cost to let you in. Or what it took to—" She stopped. Couldn't finish. "You have *no idea*."

The words hit, sharp and honest.

"That's not—" I started, but the words died in my throat. Because what could I say? That I had reasons? That it was complicated? That I was scared?

None of it mattered. I left. That was the fact.

"You made yourself vulnerable for me." The words stuttered out. "You let me in and I just—I fucking left. Without a word. Without even—" I couldn't finish. Tried again. "I can't even imagine what that—how fucked-up—" My hands didn't know what to do with themselves. Typical. "I'm sorry. Shiloh, I'm so sorry."

My chest felt like it was caving in. I blinked hard, looked at the floor, at the cables, at anything but her face. If I looked at her, I was going to crack completely, and I couldn't. Not here, not now, not when I'd already stressed her out too much.

I deserved this. Every second of her ice, every wall she'd built. I'd left, and she'd learned to live without me, and now I was here asking her to feel something she'd spent years getting over.

She looked past me, exhausted, toward the booth. "You want to do another take?"

I almost said no. I almost said something else. Instead, I nodded.

"Yeah," I said. "Let's do it."

She moved first, flicked the session back to zero, cued up the track.

I walked into the booth, pulled the headphones on, stared at my reflection until it stopped looking like me.

Four years. I'd tried to find this with other people. The way Shiloh could gut me with three sentences and make me thank her for it. Looked for it in strangers, in Skye's bed, anywhere that wasn't here. Never found it. Because you can't replace someone who learned your language before you even knew you were speaking it.

The talkback clicked on.

Shiloh's voice, soft this time. "Whenever you're ready."

I closed my eyes. Breathed in, then out. I let the pain, the anger, the fucking hunger for something real roll through me like a fever.

Pick A Struggle, Shi

Shiloh

THE CONFERENCE ROOM WAS so cold my fingers went numb after five minutes. Glass walls, glass table, glass water bottles lined up with the labels all facing forward—every detail calibrated to prove a point about money, not comfort. I saw my reflection in the window opposite: sharp jaw, collar buttoned to the top, hands folded like I was bracing for a deposition. Next to me, Bishop radiated the opposite energy, slouched so deep in her chair she looked like she might slide off the end and vanish under the table. She wore a bone-white hoodie, half-zipped, a chain glinting in the gap above her collarbone. The hood was up, framing her face and making the sunglasses look even bigger.

Chelsea from the label had the head seat. Hair slicked down and blazer pin-straight, iPad out and already logging minutes before the meeting started. The A&R, Drew, tried to set a "chill" tone by unbuttoning his cuffs and calling everyone by their artist names like we were at a group therapy session. It wasn't working. No one had said anything not directly related to scheduling in the last six minutes.

There was silence, and then Chelsea toggled the playlist on her iPad. "Let's just get right into it," she said, sliding the Bluetooth up to the room's sound system. The first notes of the "False Signal" demo rolled out—bare, high on nerves, with Bishop's voice coming in two bars late, just like she'd left it on the file. My chest went tight for a second, but I masked it by adjusting the crease on my sleeve.

Drew listened with what he must have thought was a "producer face," but it read more like someone holding in a sneeze. He drummed his fingers on the glass, nodding along, then pointed at the ceiling right as Bishop came in on the pre-chorus. "This is the part, right here, where I feel it just lifts—" He let the track run, glancing at the rest of us as if to make sure we were hearing what he heard.

Chelsea was silent, thumbs working the iPad, probably logging time-codes and quotes for the meeting transcript. I kept my eyes on the opposite window, watching Bishop's sunglasses in the reflection. She looked bored, but the hood shadowed her face so I couldn't really see.

The chorus hit, and the room seemed to shrink. Bishop's voice in the demo was unpolished, almost ragged, but she'd left every breath in. I remembered the night we'd tracked it—her jaw so tense it barely moved, the way she'd refused to run another take even when I told her the last one clipped. The rawness was the point, and I knew that if the label made her retake it, she'd burn the whole album before she did it twice.

When the track faded, silence crashed in. Chelsea didn't move for a full two seconds. Drew was the first to break, spreading his hands. "This is exactly the energy we've been chasing—grit, urgency, real narrative. You two have undeniable chemistry, it just..." He trailed off, searching for a word. "It just *bleeds* through, you know?"

I nodded, though I didn't know what he thought was bleeding. Bishop made no move at all. She didn't even pretend to smile.

Drew kept talking. "It's like you're finishing each other's sentences, but with music instead of words. I love it." He made a little prayer-hands gesture. "That's what the audience connects with, and it's what's going to push this album through. You two speak the same language, maybe more than anyone else on the roster."

There was a pause, and I realized he was waiting for me to agree out loud. "Yeah," I said. "We work well together."

Chelsea looked up, eyes ping-ponging between us, then back down to her screen. "The chorus is a little hot, but we can smooth that in post," she said. "Otherwise, this is the strongest vocal take I've heard so far. Real pain, real story."

Bishop said nothing. She'd been iced out for four days, ever since the session. The weirdest part was, the less we talked, the better the tracks got. Every time we left a session, I'd tell myself to dial it down, keep it business, and every time she came back with something more brutal, more alive. If there was a science to emotional whiplash, we'd just invented it.

Drew reset the playlist, starting the track again at the bridge. "Can we talk about this section, where the tempo drops?" He nodded at me, like I was the only one in the room. "Shiloh, you did some real magic here with the production. It's like the floor drops out, but the vocals hold it together. Is that something you can replicate on the rest of the record?"

I shifted in the chair, careful to keep my voice neutral. "It only works if the vocal's carrying enough weight. Otherwise, it just sounds empty."

Chelsea nodded. "It's Bishop's best register. When she's really pushing against the emptiness, it lands." Her eyes flicked up, this time settling on Bishop for half a second, then back to the notes.

Drew went on, "I think the fans are going to see this as a new side of you, Bishop. It's like we get to the core. More vulnerable." He waited, eager for a reaction.

Bishop lifted her chin, finally. The sunglasses made her unreadable, but her voice was flatter than old soda. "It's just a song, Drew."

He smiled like a snarl. "That's what makes it real, right?"

Bishop shrugged. "If you say so."

She made songs out of her life to understand it. That was how she survived. I'd watched her do it a thousand times. But not now. Now she was just gone.

Chelsea was the only one who seemed to notice. Her pen stilled, tablet resting flat on the table. "You okay with the release timeline, then?" she said, flipping to the calendar app. "We need a finalized comp on Friday, with the video shoot on the twenty-eighth. Shiloh, you think the rest of the tracks can land before then?"

"Easily," I said. "Half are in post. The other half need more vocals."

Chelsea nodded, making the note. "If you run into logistics issues, let me know. I'll clear her schedule for you."

Drew tapped the table. "Let's get promo working early this cycle, yeah? Once we have this bridge on lock, I want to ship it out to test audiences. Fizzr first, then a full rollout."

"Copy," I said.

They talked through logistics—press calls, remote interviews, the next three weeks mapped to the minute. Bishop didn't say a word until the end, when Chelsea asked about the draft for her own liner notes.

"They're done," Bishop said. "Check your email."

Drew leaned in, big smile. "You're a machine," he said, like it was a compliment.

She didn't answer.

When the meeting finally wrapped, Drew gathered his papers and beamed at us. "You two are gold. This is the project to beat, trust me." He stood, checked his hair in the window, then left without waiting for a response.

I sat for a few seconds, watching my reflection darken as the sun fell behind the neighboring building. My hands were still cold, knuckles gone pale where I'd gripped a pen. I tried to think of something to say, but every phrase sounded too clinical or too raw. I wanted to tell Bishop she'd nailed the take; that the bridge she'd written was better than anything on the last two records; that I missed the way we used to finish each other's ideas without turning it into a contest. Instead, I said nothing.

Bishop finally stood, letting the hood fall back. She pulled the sunglasses down, exposing eyes that looked nothing like the mask she wore for the room. She met my gaze for the first time all day, and the look held—unblinking, defiant, but also a little lost. If I was going to freeze her out, she was going to make sure I saw the damage.

It lasted maybe two seconds, then she snorted. "At least we got this right." Then, right back up.

I wanted to ask if she meant the song or the strategy of never speaking unless forced. But she was already gone, kicks echoing down the glass corridor. I watched the space where she'd been for a beat longer than I meant to.

I collected my things in silence. When I stood, I caught Chelsea's reflection in the next room, watching through the wall. She didn't wave, just gave me the smallest nod. I returned it, then walked out before she took the in to ask questions I didn't feel like answering.

The parking structure under the label building always smelled like cheap paint and old tires, with a chemical undertow that stayed on your clothes until morning. My car was on the second level, wedged between a Mercedes and a Ferrari that probably belonged to the same flavor of executive. I took the stairs instead of the elevator, needing the extra time to let my head cool, or maybe just to feel my body move after two hours of sitting with my jaw clenched.

Every footstep echoed up the concrete, just a little behind the beat. Sound chasing me, refusing to let me leave the last meeting behind. I tried to replay the highlights, but my brain kept sticking on the look Bishop gave me, the two-second stare with nothing but air and years of unfinished business in it.

I unlocked the car and stood by the door, keys in hand, palms flat on the roof. The metal was still warm from the afternoon sun, but the cold air down here made my fingers ache.

She'd barely looked at me during the meeting. Professional. Careful. Everything I'd demanded from her in the studio four days ago when I finally lost it and told her exactly what it cost me to let her in before.

And she'd listened, for once. Showed up to the meeting on time, answered questions without deflecting, didn't make a single joke at my expense. Did exactly what I'd asked her to do.

So why did it feel worse?

I'd been doing this thing, I realized, where I punished Bishop for every old wound and then pretended it was about professionalism. I spent four days acting like her calls and texts were a virus, shutting her out unless the subject was strictly work. But every time she stepped in front of a mic last week, I felt it. The gap. Before I could decide not to.

It was self-defeating. I knew it. But the alternative—letting her back in—felt like worse than a relapse.

Couldn't have it both ways. Pick a struggle, Ellis.

A pair of headlights swept through the structure, painting long shadows across the wall. I glanced up, saw Bishop at the top of the ramp, hoodie still up, walking slow and alone. Her car was three rows over, but she saw me too. For a second I thought about ducking inside and driving off, but the inertia of the day pinned me in place.

"Bishop," I said, voice sharp in the echo chamber.

She didn't answer, but turned, hands deep in her pockets, and made her way over. When she stopped in front of me, it was with a gap between us that could have held a second car.

She waited, not making it easy.

I took a breath. "About the other night," I started. "I crossed a line."

She tensed slightly, like she wasn't sure where this was going. "Which one?"

"Using your name like that." I kept my voice level. "It was unprofessional. I made it personal when it should've stayed about the work."

She was quiet for a moment, studying my face. "And now you want to take it back."

"I want to establish boundaries," I said. "Clean ones. So we can finish this album without—" I stopped, recalibrated. What, killing each other? "Without complications."

Or feeling like I'm about to combust when she gets too close. That might be nice.

"Complications." She said it flat, testing the weight of the word. "They loved the complications in there."

I didn't follow. "What?"

"The A&R guy. Chelsea. They loved the track. The messy one." She shifted her weight. "The one that came from all this—" She gestured between us. "Whatever this is."

It landed wrong in my gut—whatever this is—like she was naming something I'd been carefully stepping around for days. My keys dug into my palm. I looked past her shoulder at the concrete pillar behind her, the oil stain on the ground, anywhere but her face.

"That doesn't mean—"

"Maybe the mess is part of it," she said. "Maybe trying to clean it up is what's fucking us up."

It was so Bishop, but there wasn't any heat in it. Just a tired truth. For once, she wasn't trying to win. She was just trying to be heard.

I hated that she was right. The more I tried to box her out, the better the work got. It made no sense, unless you understood us. I looked at the parking lines, at the oil slicks on the concrete, at anything but her.

"It can't be about us," I said, finally. "It has to be about the record."

It tasted familiar. Safe.

Bishop's jaw worked for a second, like she was chewing on words she didn't want to swallow. "Look, I know I pushed too hard, too. Kept bringing up shit you didn't want to talk about." She shifted, uncomfortable. "I get why you're pissed."

"Yeah," I said. Just that.

She didn't say sorry. Couldn't quite make herself say it. But the acknowledgment was out there anyway. Bishop nodded, hands still buried in her pockets. "Yeah, okay. The record. That's what you want?"

The question had weight I wasn't ready for. Almost felt as if she was asking something else entirely.

I nodded. "We'll hit the bridge Monday. Same time."

For a second, I thought she might say something else—something like sorry, or maybe just goodbye. But she just turned and walked away.

Halfway to her truck, she slowed. Almost stopped. Didn't.

I got in my car, sat with the engine off, and let the silence pile up.

Somewhere overhead, another car door slammed, then nothing.

I sat there until whatever was sitting heavy on my chest got up. Then I started the engine, let the radio fill the void, and drove.

I drove until the city started to blur together—strip malls, vape shops, bars, and then the brick-walled galleries of the Art District. At six p.m. on a Thursday, the light was already blue, casting everything in that fake Pixogram glow that made LA look more interesting than it really was. I didn't have a destination, just a need to keep moving so my brain wouldn't catch up to itself.

At the stoplight on 7th, I watched an art student couple wait at the crosswalk. The girl knocked her shoulder into her friend, laughing at something, easy and uncomplicated. They crossed without looking back.

My hands tightened on the wheel.

You don't resist what pulls you naturally.

But I'd spent four years doing exactly that.

I pulled into Thai Number Nine because my body knew the route even when my brain had checked out. Ordered the usual. Sat by the window with my receipt, watching people live their lives—probably going home to someone, or a cat, not carrying around four years of scar tissue disguised as boundaries.

The food came. I paid. Drove home on autopilot.

Inside my apartment, everything was exactly as I'd left it: clean, controlled, floral. I sat at the kitchen table with the takeout container, eating without tasting, while the silence pressed in from all sides.

I pushed the drunken noodles around, suddenly not hungry.

Monday was another session. We'd make another track that sounded like two people bleeding out. The label would love it. When we were done, I'd go home intact, financially secure, and completely alone. Ready for the next project.

Professional. Boundaried. Safe.

The words sat in my mouth like cold coffee.

My phone was face-up on the table. No notifications. I willed it to light up, then hated myself for wanting it to.

She wasn't going to text. Why would she? I'd been clear about what I wanted.

Except I hadn't been clear at all.

Maybe I was just lonely. It had been a while since I'd let anyone close, and Bishop had been keeping herself plenty busy with Skye. Maybe I was making my own dry spell her problem. Projecting need onto someone who'd already found what she wanted elsewhere. This was why I should've said no to the album. Bishop had already moved on, and here I was, making shit weird.

I picked up my phone. Put it down. Picked it up again.

Our text thread was a graveyard of professional efficiency. Just scheduling and confirmations. Not even a stupid, long rambling voice note from her about the last session.

I scrolled back to five years ago. Found one from a Saturday night:

> *u tapped out at level 8. im the hot ones*

Her reply:

My chest went heavy again. Heavier.

I could text her. Could say something true.

I miss you. I'm watching you disappear, and I want the mess back.

But what if she didn't want that anymore? What if today was the moment she finally learned to let me go?

I locked the phone. Set it down.

The apartment felt smaller. My diffuser smelled wrong. Too sweet, trying too hard. I thought about opening a window but didn't move.

Monday. Four days from now. I'd know by how she looked at me—or didn't—whether I'd finally succeeded in pushing her away for good.

But tonight, I sat in my too-clean apartment, drowning in the safety I'd asked for, wondering when "professional" started feeling like a prison sentence.

No peace, just quiet.

Okay, Track Four Might Be About You

Bishop

A WEEK SINCE SHE'D called me Evienne and went clean off on me.

Not that I was counting.

I showed up early—first time in my life—because sitting in my apartment was worse than facing her. At least at the studio there was a chance she'd look at me. At home, there was just the phone I kept checking for a text that never came.

The door was unlocked. She was already there, of course. Probably had been for hours.

"Hey," I said, too casual, like my heart wasn't trying to break my ribs.

She glanced up. Nodded. "We're working on 'Cathedral' tonight. Label wants it tighter."

And there it was. That voice. The one that made whole rooms shut up and fall in line. Four years gone and my body still didn't know how to act right when she used that voice. Pulse doing whatever it wanted, loud as a kick drum.

"Yeah, okay." I looked somewhere else. Anywhere else.

The problem revealed itself immediately: only one chair at the console, plush carpet next to it, and we needed to review the waveforms together. I looked around for something to drag over, but there was only hers. The second chair had been relocated. Convenient. Shiloh was already pulling up the session, clearly expecting me to just...figure shit out.

There was a whole suite worth of chairs I could've gone looking for. I looked at the carpet instead.

Fuck it.

I kneeled. Dropped down beside her chair like it was the most natural thing in the world, like I hadn't just put myself physically below her, like the symbolism wasn't screaming.

If she noticed, she didn't say anything. Just pulled up the track and hit play.

"I confess, I confess, I confess—"

My voice, raw and wrecked, filled the room. I'd recorded this right after she'd gutted me. Every word was a wound I'd sung into the mic because I couldn't say it to her face.

"The reverb's too wet here," Shiloh said, clinical, pointing at the screen. "Muddies the consonants. We'll have to do it again."

I was close enough to smell the lavender. Close enough to see the inside of her wrist. Close enough to count her breaths.

"Yeah," I managed. "Too wet."

She made the adjustment, soloed my vocal, played it back. Her hand was steady on the mouse. Mine were folded in my lap.

We listened to the track just like that. Me on my knees, her in the chair, our shoulders almost touching when she'd lean forward. Every time she moved, I felt it like electricity.

Small moments started stacking:

I made a joke about the compression—something dumb about choking the life out of my voice—and her mouth twitched. Almost a smile. Almost.

She reached for the keyboard at the same time I reached for the mouse. Our hands touched. She didn't pull away immediately.

"What were you thinking here?" she asked, pointing at a phrase I'd sung off tempo. "This section—what did you mean?"

It was a producer question. Technical. But the way she asked it felt like more.

"I meant—" I stopped, looked at the waveform like it had answers. "I was thinking about Harmony Heights. About the last session we did before I signed."

She went very still. "Oh."

"Yeah."

She knew what I meant. We'd never talked about that night. What I'd said, how she'd looked at me after. I walked out of that studio and didn't see her again for four years, and it was still sitting there between us. This album had an end date too. Then what? Another four years? Back to acting like we never made each other laugh in the booth at 2 a.m.?

She played that part again. The phrase felt heavier every time I heard it: "I confess I don't know how to stay."

"Bishop—"

"I know I fucked up," I blurted. Couldn't hold it anymore. "I know I left, and I know I hurt you, and I know showing up here four years later asking you to—to—" I made hand movements helplessly at the space between us. "I don't know! I don't fucking know, okay? I just know this—" Another gesture, more desperate. "—feels wrong and I don't know how to make it not wrong."

Silence. My heart was trying to escape my chest. I was still on my knees, looking up at her, completely exposed.

Shiloh turned in the chair. Faced me fully.

She'd been leaning closer. The distance kept shrinking, but now she was right there. Close enough I could see the exact shade of brown in her eyes. The same look she'd given me that first time, in the Harmony Heights control room at 3 a.m. She'd looked at me like she was deciding something before she kissed me back. When she'd cupped my face and kissed me against the wall, soft and sure, everything changed between us.

She'd chosen me then. Risked everything for me then.

Her hand lifted. Deliberate.

Her thumb touched my lips. Not covering my mouth completely. Resting there against my bottom lip, at the corner of my mouth. Silencing me. Claiming me. Devastating me.

I stopped breathing.

The touch was so controlled. Everything Shiloh did was like that, economical and sure. Just her thumb on my mouth and her eyes locked on mine, and my entire body went hot and liquid. This was what I'd been missing. Not just her, but this—the way she could end a conversation with a single gesture, the way she took up space without ever raising her voice.

God, I'd tried to replace this. Found people who had to work for it, who needed you to know. Shiloh wasn't doing anything. Just sitting there, four years of distance still on her face, and I couldn't get up.

"You're telling me you're uncomfortable," she said, voice low. I couldn't see her eyes behind the lights in her glasses anymore. "I've been uncomfortable for four years."

The pause stretched. Her thumb pressed slightly, like she was feeling the shape of my mouth, remembering it.

"But I hear you."

I couldn't move. Couldn't breathe. Her hand was on my lips, and I was on my knees, and the studio was so quiet I could hear both our hearts racing, or maybe that was just mine, trying to punch through my ribs.

Her eyes dropped to where she rested against my mouth. Just for a second. Then back to my eyes.

I parted my lips. Barely. Just enough to feel her ridges of skin against the sensitive inside edge, enough to taste the salt of her fingertips.

Her breath caught. I heard it.

"Shiloh—" I whispered against her hand.

She leaned down. Slow, like she was still deciding, like she could still stop this. But she didn't stop.

Her hand slid from my mouth to cup my chin, angling my face up, and then her lips were on mine and the world fucking ended.

It wasn't soft. Wasn't gentle. If anything, it was four years of anger and want and grief, all forced down into a pinprick, a collision that cracked me open. Her mouth claimed mine with that voltage—a punishing hunger, not asking permission, not even pretending to be gentle. I didn't hesitate, I just opened for her, greedy, desperate, a sound coming up from somewhere inside me. Should've been embarrassing. Wasn't.

I reached up—hands shaking, grabbing at her thighs, her hips, trying to pull her closer even though she was already as close as physics allowed with me on the floor and her in the chair. She made a sound too, low and broken, and her other hand buried itself in my hair, gripping hard enough to hurt.

Good. I wanted it to hurt. Wanted proof this was real and happening.

She kissed me like she was trying to get something back that I'd stolen. Like she was furious and hungry and desperate all at once. I kissed her back like an apology, like a confession, like the only honest thing I'd ever done.

When she finally pulled back—not far, just enough to breathe—her forehead dropped against mine. Her hand was still in my hair. Mine were still clutching her like a lifeline.

"Fuck," she breathed.

"Yeah," I said, or tried to. It came out wrecked.

We stayed like that, breathing each other's air, neither of us willing to be the first to let go.

Her thumb stroked along my jaw, almost gentle now. "This doesn't fix anything."

"I know."

"This is still a terrible idea."

"God, I know."

"We still have to finish this album."

I said it against her lips. "Let me have you."

She pulled back enough to look at me. Her lips were swollen. Her eyes were dark. She looked as ruined as I felt.

"We shouldn't—"

I kissed her again before she could finish the thought. Couldn't help it. Needed it more than air.

This time she let me lead, let me pour four years of I'm sorry, and I missed you, and please don't give up on me, into the press of mouth against mouth. Her fingers tightened in my hair, and she made that sound again, the one that went straight through me.

When we broke apart this time, I was the one who pulled back. Just far enough to see her face.

"I fucked up," I said. Raw. Honest. "I left and I shouldn't have and I've been—" My voice cracked. "I've been trying to figure out how to tell you I'm sorry for four years, and I still don't know how."

She looked at me for a long moment. Her hand loosened in my hair, slid down to cup my face.

"You just did."

The words hung between us, permission and warning all at once.

"Want you," I said. Simple. True. No metaphor, no joke to hide behind. Just the raw admission I'd been choking on for days. Weeks. Years.

Her eyes darkened. Her thumb traced my bottom lip, still swollen from kissing her.

"Bishop—"

"Don't call me Bishop. Not right now." I said, voice breaking on my name.

Something shifted in her face. Cracked open.

"E," she drew it out, testing it. Tasting it. Remembering how it used to sound in her mouth.

I nodded, not trusting my voice anymore.

She stood up. For a horrible second, I thought she was leaving, thought I'd pushed too far, said too much. But then her hands were on my shoulders, pulling me up from my knees.

"Stand up."

I did, shaky, and suddenly we were face-to-face, breathing the same air again.

"If we do this—" she started.

"We don't have to—" I tried to give her an out, even though it was killing me.

"If we do this," she continued, firmer now, "you don't get to run. Not this time."

My heart stopped. Started again, harder.

"I don't want to anymore," I said. "I promise. I—"

She kissed me again, harder this time, backing me up against the console. Equipment dug into my spine and I didn't care. Didn't care about anything except her hands on me, her mouth on mine, the way she was pressed against me like she was trying to fuse us together.

"I want you so much," she breathed against my lips.

The admission broke something in me. I kissed her harder, hands sliding under her shirt, needing skin, needing more proof I wouldn't wake up fisting the sheets again. She gasped into my mouth when my fingers found the bare skin of her waist, warm and solid and *here*.

"E—" My name was a prayer and a warning.

"Please," I said, and I wasn't above begging. Not with her. Never with her. "Need you. Right now."

She pulled back just enough to look at me, eyes searching mine for something—doubt, hesitation, the same fear that made me run last time. Whatever she saw must've satisfied her because she grabbed my hand and pulled me toward the couch.

It looked like the same couch where we used to sit for hours, working through arrangements, sharing headphones, falling asleep on each other when sessions ran too late. Now, she was pushing me down onto it, following me, settling her weight on top of me like she belonged there.

And fuck, she did. She always had.

Her mouth found my neck and I arched into her, hands fisting in her shirt, pulling her closer. She bit down—not hard enough to bruise but hard enough to make me gasp—and soothed it with her tongue.

"Still sensitive here," she murmured against my skin, and the fact that she remembered, that she knew my body like a map she'd memorized, made my eyes sting.

I grunted.

"E." She pulled back, looked down at me. Her hair was messy from my hands, lips swollen, eyes dark with want behind those glasses.

"Shiloh," I breathed, and she rewarded me with another kiss, deep and slow and thorough.

Her hands slid under my shirt, pushing it up. I sat up enough to let her pull it over my head, then reached for hers. She let me, watching me with that intense focus she got when she was working, like I was a mix she was trying to perfect.

When we were both bare from the waist up, she paused. Just looked at me.

"You got a new tattoo."

Her fingers traced the ink on my ribs. Words in her handwriting, because I'd sent the artist a screenshot of her scribbles. I'd gotten it two years ago, half-drunk and lonely and missing her so badly I couldn't breathe. (I caved and texted her. She had me blocked.)

"What?" I asked, suddenly self-conscious.

Her voice came out barely a whisper. "You put us under your heart."

I couldn't look at her. "Where else was I supposed to keep you?"

She went completely still. Then she leaned down, pressed her lips to the first word. Then the next. *Let. Me. In. While. My. Fists. Still. Believe. In. You.* Ten separate places her mouth touched my skin. I counted because I couldn't do anything else. I was breathing entirely too hard by then.

"Fuck—"

"I know." She moved up my body, kissing a path from my ribs to my collarbone to my jaw, stopping to swirl her tongue around my nipples. "I know."

Her hand slid down, popping the button on my jeans. I lifted my hips to help her pull them down, taking my boxers with them, until I was completely bare beneath her.

She sat back on her heels, still straddling me, just looking.

"Stop staring," I muttered, fighting the urge to cover myself.

"No." Her voice was rough. "Your body looks different now. I'm memorizing this. All of it."

Then her hand was between my thighs and I stopped thinking entirely.

She touched me like she was working. Careful first. Then building. Same precision as the mixing board. Listening for every response, every catch, every involuntary movement. She knew where to touch, knew how to play every note in my body. And I let her wreck me. Desperate for it. For her. For whatever sound she could pull out that was only mine with her.

"Look at me," she said, and I forced my eyes open.

She was watching my face with that producer focus, cataloging every reaction, learning what worked. It should've made me self-conscious but instead it made me hotter—her paying attention, that she cared about getting it right. The fact that she kept her glasses on was *hot*.

"Shi, please—"

"I've got you." Her thumb found my clit, and I nearly came off the couch, hips jerking up to meet her touch, trying to get more—deeper, closer. "That's it. Let me hear you."

I was making sounds I'd be embarrassed about later—needy, desperate, totally unfiltered. But she seemed to drink it in, her breathing getting heavier as mine did, her eyes locked on me like she couldn't look away.

"Fuck me," I whined. "Please."

Her mouth opened in a gasp. She sank her fingers into me, deep and sure, and my hips rolled up to take her, hungry for every inch. I cried out, clutching at her shoulders, needing her everywhere at once, forever if she'd let me. She set a rhythm—steady, deliberate—but I was the one moving now, chasing her, setting the pace with every desperate thrust.

"You really missed me, huh," she breathed, almost reverent. "I forgot how wet you get when we—"

She didn't finish. Just leaned down and kissed me while she fucked me with her hand, swallowing every sound I made. I was close, so close, teetering on the edge.

Her fingers never slowed. She leaned in, voice low and rough beside my ear. Total goosebumps. "Tell me it's mine."

My breath hitched, heat rushing in. I fucked myself on her hand, hard, pressure building.

"It's yours," I hissed. My hips ground into her fingers. "Please, Shi."

She smiled against my jaw, eyes holding that dark satisfaction like she'd just nailed the perfect take. "Good," she murmured. "Come for me. Want to feel it."

That did it. I came hard, clenching around her, her name a gasp on my lips. She worked me through it, slowing her touch as I came down, pressing soft kisses to my jaw, my neck, my shoulder.

When I could breathe again, I pulled her down and kissed her. Slower this time. Trying to say something I didn't have words for.

"Need to taste you," I said, already reaching for her jeans.

She caught my wrist. "We don't have to—"

"Shiloh." I looked her in the eye, maybe a bit wild. "I want to. Please let me."

She studied my face for a moment, then nodded.

I flipped us—clumsy, graceless, nearly falling off the couch—but managed to get her on her back. Stripped her out of her remaining clothes with shaking hands. Took a moment to just look at her.

She was beautiful. Always had been. The monitors painted her skin in blues and greens, made her look unreal. Like something I'd imagined instead of something I got to touch.

I kissed down her body—neck, collarbone, breasts, stomach—taking my time. Circled her nipples, tongued every ripple of her abs. Making up for lost years I'd tossed aside, telling myself I didn't miss this. *Her.* When I settled between her thighs, she was already wet.

She pressed her thumb back to my lips. I took it in, sucking slow and deep, eyes locked on hers. She watched, transfixed, breath hitching.

I smiled around it, then released her with a soft pop—nipping her thigh instead. Shiloh sucked in a quick breath.

I started slow, relearning her. What made her hips lift, what made her fingers tighten in my hair, what made her say my name like that—breathy and desperate and perfect.

She tasted like coming home.

My tongue circled deeper now. Lazier strokes turned insistent. Her thighs tensed around my shoulders, and she moaned, almost pained. I spread her legs wider for me.

The look on her face, like she needed this, needed me, I didn't know what to do with that except give her more. I lost myself tongue-fucking her deep. The feel of Shiloh, her desperate sounds, her taste, her smell, the way she fluttered against my mouth. She gasped low, and palmed the back of my head, pleading with her body for more. I looked up again. Shouldn't have. Shiloh was watching me through those frames, eyes half-lidded and locked on mine, nipples hard, breathing like I'd stolen all the air from her lungs.

Heat slammed between my legs with the force of a flat hand, sharp enough to make me clench.

Built her up slow, then faster when her hips stuttered, when I felt her teetering on the edge. She begged for my fingers, and I gave her what she wanted, sliding them past her swollen lips and feeling her wet grip around me—God, I'd missed this. I remembered exactly what she needed, the way she'd suck in a breath when I latched onto her clit and sucked, steady and deep, not stopping for anything. I did it now, holding her with one hand, working her until she was fucking my mouth.

Her fingers tangled in my hair, tug soft then urgent. "Right there," she gasped. I didn't change a thing. Just hummed into her skin, kept my mouth and fingers moving, steady and sure, until she was coming, hips grinding into my face. I was greedy for every drop of her.

I kissed both her thighs until she was soft, pliant, glassy-eyed. Then I crawled back up, mouth slick, and let her pull me down for a kiss. Slow, syrup-sweet, and brutal. Nothing ever did it for me like kissing her right after, letting her taste herself on me, showing her how much she always lost the last of her chill with me between her legs. I loved reminding her of who the fuck I was.

We lay there for a while, breathing hard and stuck together on the too-small couch. Our skin cooling in the studio's recycled air. Her hands were warm on my back. Mine played with her hair. I didn't want to move an inch, be separated from her ever again.

"This doesn't solve everything."

"I *know*, Shi."

She was quiet for a moment. "But it's a start."

I pressed a kiss to her shoulder and she turned, found my mouth with hers. Still hungry, still not ready to stop. Breathing with each other. We stayed there, wrapped up in each other, no one reaching for clothes, no one willing to end this yet.

The knock came, sharp and sudden. Fucking perfect timing.

"Janitorial!"

Shiloh jerked, breathless. "Occupied!" she called out, voice shaky, barely pulling her mouth from mine.

We both froze. Listened to the footsteps fade down the hall. Adrenaline buzzing between us, the moment cracked but not shattered yet.

A Day in the Life

Shiloh

I WOKE TO THE feel of warm skin under my cheek, an ache between my legs, and the weight of an unfamiliar comfort pinning me to the mattress.

The light was all wrong—filtered gold through horizontal blinds, falling in stripes across the foot of a bed. My bed for the night, apparently. I registered all of this with a slow contentment before the memory of last night hit in full: the cleaning crew's keys jingling outside the studio door, the scramble to pull ourselves together, the muffled laughter up the stairs, the race back to her place to finish what we started, her weight warm and heavy over me. Pressure somewhere new. Legs almost quit in protest by the time we were done. Turns out that new body came with all kinds of stamina that should be illegal.

Adrenaline spiked my pulse in the half second before I realized whose breath was slow and steady against the back of my neck.

Bishop's arm was draped over my hip, her palm open and slack against my thigh. I'd ended up with most of the covers but none of my dignity, wearing nothing but her T-shirt—oversized, faded, so old the tag was blank. It still smelled faintly of that expensive cologne she always wore. It wasn't the first time I'd slept in her clothes. Just the first time in four years.

I shifted, careful not to wake her. She made a sound, low and soft, and burrowed closer, her fingers tightening just enough to remind me she was there. I let myself drift, cataloging the strange familiarity of her bedroom. The sheets were expensive too—high thread count, warm from her body, already twisted into a spiral at the foot of the bed. The comforter was halfway on the floor. Piles of clothes—hers and mine, mixed together—dripped off the backs of chairs and bled into each other along the baseboards. There were stacks of Michael Jackson vinyl records against the wall, some in milk crates, some just leaning like they'd been set down mid-rush and never picked back up. More than a dozen notebooks scattered across the dresser, some closed, some split open, paper wilted from heavy ink. A single sneaker, bright orange, lay on its side next to the row of floating sneaker racks. The place looked like a high-end thrift store had been ransacked by a tornado. Nothing matched, nothing was in its place, and somehow the room felt more like a home than anywhere I'd lived in a decade, even back in New York.

My apartment was neat, organized, predictable. Every surface dusted and every cable labeled. I liked control. I liked knowing that if I reached for something it would be exactly where I'd left it, nothing shifting beneath my feet. But lying here, in the unmade bed of a woman who thrived on chaos, I felt a kind of peace I couldn't remember ever allowing myself.

I turned on my back, careful not to dislodge her arm. Bishop was still out cold, mouth parted just enough to catch the light on her stud earring. She looked different asleep—less chaotic, more calm. Fifteen years I'd known this face. Four years I'd tried to forget it. The lines at the corners of her eyes were deeper now, but the rest was pure Evienne. I watched her for a long time, letting myself have this quiet, unguarded version of her before she woke up.

She woke anyway, with a series of micro-movements—a twitch of her fingers, a slow inhale, the careful way her eyelids fluttered open as if the morning might be a trick. She met my gaze with a flat, unblinking stare. For a split second I feared every possible reaction that might cross her face: denial, bravado, panic, hunger. In the end, it was none of those. She just looked at me, tired and real, and let out a sigh.

"Look at you being a creeper," she said, her voice nothing like the weapon she used in public—just gravel and sleep.

Guess I was watching her sleep, wasn't I? "Morning to you too, E."

There was a long, weighty pause. The kind that made you remember everything you'd said and done the night before, every word and touch and confession.

Then Bishop, of course, shattered it. She looked at my barely covered ass. "If you're gonna run, do it now. But at least let me watch first."

I snorted, then immediately regretted it—my head was splitting in three different directions. "Not running."

"Good." She propped herself up on one elbow, gaze drifting again to the way her T-shirt covered my thighs. "You make that look better than me. Unfair."

I rolled my eyes but couldn't help the heat crawling up my neck. "I'm sure you'll be fine."

"Barely." Bishop collapsed back to the pillow, arm flung dramatically across her face. Her mouth curved into a smile under the crook of her elbow.

I wedged my leg between hers, bare mound on her hip.

She slid her arm behind her head and turned to me. "Careful, or you might become breakfast."

I didn't move. Didn't want to. The silence that fell between us was less about avoidance than absorption. I curled into her warmth. We'd said what we needed to last night. Now it was just the two of us, blinking into the daylight, trying to decide if the spell would hold when the world woke up.

After a while, Bishop reached over and tangled her fingers in mine. Her grip was loose, but insistent. Like she needed the anchor. I understood.

We lay like that for a long time, trading warmth and listening to the city build momentum outside the windows. She traced circles on my knuckles. I mapped her hand over mine.

I thought of how much I used to hate this: these slow, useless mornings, time spent not doing when my brain was running in different directions. But with Bishop, even stillness felt like movement. There was always a current under the surface, waiting to pull us under if we looked away too long.

Eventually, she broke the quiet. "I have a shoot at noon. If I don't show up, they're threatening to Photoshop my entire head on someone else's body."

I hummed. "Lunch meeting at one. Cam's A&R wants to talk timeline, push the singles before the winter grant deadline."

Bishop stiffened. "You're seeing Cam?"

"It's a business lunch, not a date," I said, squeezing her fingers. "You'll be fine."

She grinned, sharp and bright. "You think so? Because if you show up to that meeting with those hickeys, I'm going to get side-eye at every industry thing from now to next year."

I froze. "Hickeys—"

"C'mere." She pulled the covers aside, inspecting my neck with exaggerated seriousness. "Mmmm. Maybe one or two. Possibly three."

I tried to glare, but she kissed me on the neck, soft and close-mouthed. Her lips brushed each spot she'd marked; I almost forgot what we were talking about.

It was our first almost-kiss moment all over again. Her pinning me under her, breathing hard, except this time I was brave. Back then, Bishop had named what was happening between us, dared me to meet her there. This time, I did. I took her face in my hands and kissed her. Nothing careful and certainly not coy, either. Just need, plain and blunt. She smiled against my mouth, slow and a little surprised, and I pressed closer, memorizing the taste of her, the shape of her breath. For a second, it was so easy to lose myself in the heat of it, the morning light, the quiet promise that maybe we could have this—just for now, just like this. Not all the painful shit and the silence after.

Words piled up in my head. Clarifications, disclaimers. The weight of it was getting old.

When she drew back, her eyes were clear and unguarded. They almost ached to look at. Fingers trailed down my face. "Last night wasn't a mistake, Shi. Don't let your brain fuck it up."

I swallowed, taking in the peace offered instead. "Wasn't planning to."

"Good." She nudged my shoulder. "Get up. I'll make you the worst coffee you've ever had."

I sat up, the sheets falling into my lap. Bishop watched me with naked appreciation—no filter, no attempt at subtlety. She liked what she saw, and she wanted me to know it.

I found my pants tangled at the foot of the bed, pulled them on, and followed her to the kitchen. The apartment opened into a living area that was equal parts studio, crash pad, and minor art installation. The kitchen counter was home to a mound of unopened mail.

Bishop handed me a mug—ceramic, black, emblazoned with WORLD'S OKAYEST GOD in gold script—and started the coffee. I perched on the stool next to the counter, feet tucked up, clutching the mug like it could anchor me to this moment. I watched her move around the kitchen: loose, unselfconscious, already composing lyrics in her head, if the muttering under her breath was any sign.

She caught me looking. "What?"

"Nothing."

She fixed me with a look that dared me to keep it to myself.

So I didn't. "You're happier here than you were in New York."

She snorted. "Low bar, Ellis."

"Even so," I said. "You are."

For a moment she didn't respond, just poured the coffee into my mug. She leaned against the counter next to me, her thigh pressing into mine, eyes on the floor.

"I am," she said finally, looking me in the eye. She paused, mouth working around the words like they tasted foreign. Kissed my shoulder. "Now, anyway."

I set my mug down, wrapped my arms around her waist, squeezed.

We drank our coffee in silence, letting the day build around us, not ready to leave the eye of the storm. I could've stayed like this forever, but my phone buzzed a reminder for the meeting—a calendar alert, ugly and insistent, breaking the spell.

I stood, drained the last of my coffee, and started gathering my things. Bishop followed me back to the bedroom, arms folded like she was bracing for impact.

At the door, she blocked my way. "Promise me something."

I cocked an eyebrow. "We're doing promises now?"

"Promise me you'll come back tonight?" She paused, then added, "I mean—not in a clingy way. In a 'don't make me eat takeout alone like a sad divorced dad' way."

The question settled between us, heavier than anything we'd said last night.

I nodded. "I'll come back."

Her relief was visible. She leaned in and kissed me—quick, hard, desperate. I let her. Probably needed it as much as she did. More.

Then she let me go.

The sunlight was blinding in the hallway. I took the stairs, pulse still racing, already replaying the shape of her hand on my skin, the after-image of her lips against mine.

I didn't know if I believed in fresh starts. But walking to my car, I let myself believe in the possibility. Just for a minute. Just long enough to get me through the day.

My apartment was quiet when I got home. Too quiet. After last night's chaos—Bishop's hands, Bishop's mouth, the noise we'd made together—the silence felt deliberate. Engineered.

I dropped my keys in the tray, caught my reflection in the hallway mirror while getting ready for the meeting. The bruise on my neck was dark enough to show above my collar. She'd marked me on purpose.

Her text came while I was at the kitchen counter:

I stared at that bat emoji longer than I should have. Typed back something about revoking studio privileges. She'd called it squatter's rights. I was still grinning when I locked my phone and headed out.

The restaurant was all dark wood and chrome art installations, expensive but tasteful. My reservation was for 1:00, but Cam's A&R was already waiting, eyeing the entrance like she expected an ambush.

I recognized her from LinkedIn. Sharp undercut, thin gold hoops, the air of someone who could end you with a handshake. Peach pantsuit, no shirt underneath, but she wore it like armor.

"Shiloh Ellis." She stood, extending her hand. Her grip was exactly as lethal as advertised. "Asha Patel. Glad you could make it."

"Good spot," I said, matching her energy but not her aggression.

"Cam's call. She likes the fries." Asha slid back into her seat, already waving for water. "She'll be late. Always is."

I pulled up my contract notes on the tablet. "Should we start?"

"Might as well."

We covered the basics: Q1 release window, pre-production logistics. Asha kept one eye on her phone, fielding texts like she was coordinating airstrikes.

"Cam's excited to work with you again," Asha said. "Feels bad about the leak last time."

"Cam's easy to work with," I said, sidestepping the leak. The industry loved to spill tea, and it was too messy for me. "She knows what she wants."

Asha's eyebrows lifted. "You're the only producer who's ever called her easy."

"She's direct. I remember that from before. Nightmare is when they want you to guess."

That landed. Asha's posture softened.

"Her new vision is"—Asha made air quotes—"'indie disco gospel.' No idea what that means, but she swears you're the only one who can do it."

I suppressed a laugh at the mental image. "I can work with that. I'll have her send over reference tracks."

At 1:14, Cam walked in. No entourage, no fanfare, just a dark denim jacket, comfy jeans, and a baby blue mesh shirt that showed off the tattoos on her neck. She spotted us, threw up a two-finger salute, and slid into the booth next to Asha.

"Am I late?" Cam asked, not actually apologizing.

"Always."

The three of us worked through a shared plate of plantain chips, building the session plan and picking apart what Cam's label would expect from the singles. At some point, Asha started taking calls at the bar, leaving me and Cam to catch up.

"Real talk," Cam said, dipping a fry in aioli. "I saw a ton of buzz on Pixogram about you working on the new album. The art kids are losing it. That shit's real?"

"It's happening," I said, keeping my tone neutral.

"Wild," she said. "Didn't think she'd go full-on weird girl. Always pegged her as a banger machine, not a poet."

"Ev—Bishop is both," I said, trying to keep the pride out of my voice.

Cam's eyes narrowed, but she didn't call me out. "She's got some next-level stuff on the way. There's been, like, ten react videos already."

I shrugged. "You know how hype cycles work. I just engineer it."

Cam grinned, all teeth. "Sure you do."

We let the silence stretch for a bit, both pretending to focus on the fries.

"You two ever get over the Harmony Heights thing?" she asked, quieter.

I looked at her. Cam had shown up during the studio's last year—after leaving her R&B group, the one with Skye. She'd been chasing something rawer, more experimental that didn't confine her words to song breaks. Found Harmony Heights right as it was dying. She'd seen enough to know what Bishop and I had been building, but she'd missed the good years. Missed when it felt like we were two music nerds creating something that could last.

Six months after Bishop signed her deal with Peachtree, the building got sold. Turned into luxury lofts, and I never got over seeing my studio equipment moved out under blankets when Dad let it go. He didn't have baller money anymore and was no longer willing to fund a nepo baby's dream. Harmony Heights died the way a lot of artist spaces do—not with a bang, just a quiet eviction notice and some venture capitalist's renovation plans.

"We're working together," I said. Not an answer.

Cam's mouth quirked. "That is not what I asked."

I paused. "Depends on the day."

Cam sipped her water. "She's a lot. You're a lot, too, but in a different way."

"Thanks?"

"It's a compliment," she said, then caught herself. "Shit, that sounded—look, I'm not trying to overstep. We put all that shit behind us. You know I care about you, right? Like, genuinely." The words tumbled faster, that run-on enthusiasm kicking in even when she was nervous. "I'ma keep it a buck—Bishop's fucking brilliant. She's magnetic. But she's also the kind of person who pulls you right in and then vanishes when shit gets real. And you deserve someone who stays. You have to know that, Shi."

She tapped her fingers slightly, all that nervous energy leaking out. "That's all I'm saying. As a friend. Who has seen some shit and doesn't want to watch you go through that again."

She was trying to be kind, but her words hit a little too close to the white meat.

"Fuck. Sorry. That was—" She ran a hand through her hair. "I should shut up now."

Cam made everything seem simple. I wondered, not for the first time, if we could've worked out. If simple would've ever been enough for me.

Already knew the answer.

I took a drink. "I'll try not to."

Cam studied me for a moment, something knowing in her expression, then let it go. "Good."

I swallowed down the instinct to snap back, to ask outright if she knew Bishop was still seeing Skye—if I'd spent last night in her bed, were there rules I needed to know?

I wanted to make it clear: If we're doing this, it's just us. No one else. But what claim did I really have, after all these years and all that distance? This thing between us was barely new, barely real outside the studio. I didn't know what I was allowed to ask for, or if wanting more already made me foolish. So instead, I just nodded, stuck to the business at hand as my stomach sank, just a little.

Asha returned, looking frazzled. "Sorry—crisis averted. Cam, we've got to bounce in ten if you want to make the interview."

Cam fist bumped me and slid out of the booth. "See ya later, Shi."

Asha offered another bone-crusher handshake, then left with Cam trailing after.

I paid for my iced coffee, stepped out into the blinding afternoon. My phone vibrated, an email alert.

I unlocked it to find three new emails. The first was from the label. Subject line in all caps:

URGENT: RADIO, CLEAN, FIZZR EDITS NEEDED BY TO-MORROW MORNING

Three different cuts of the Bishop single, all cleared for content by 10 a.m. PST. No mention of compensation for the rush.

I locked my phone and headed for the car. The day was already too bright, headache forming at my temples, but for once it felt like the good kind. Something to build on. Distract. One of those things.

The playlist shuffled to some bass-heavy track with harps I'd had on repeat for days. For a split second, I let myself believe in the possibility of this—whatever we were calling us now. That maybe, this time, she'd stick around long enough to see what happened next.

The studio was quiet when I unlocked the steel door. No Bishop humming off-key, no sneakers squeaking across laminate, no "Shiiii, can you fix my levels?" from the booth. Just the low hum of electricity and the weight of missing her.

Four years of missing the chaos.

I turned on the overheads. The gear rack blinked to life—LEDs pulsing, meters waking up. I hung my jacket, opened the session file for "Glass Stain Boys."

Post-production doesn't give a shit if you're tired, or if your last memory of the artist is their mouth pressed to your throat. It just wants clean edits and zero mistakes.

I set my laptop on the mixing desk, phone face-down. The air still smelled like lavender, but Bishop's cologne was gone, like someone had intentionally wiped away the evidence.

For the first half hour, it worked. I cut stems, ran de-essers, spot-checked for FCC violations. Bishop's vocal was raw and perfect. I started the first of three versions.

My phone vibrated. I ignored it for two minutes before checking.

> *Shoot's a clusterfuck. will text when we're clear, don't wait up*

I replied:

> *No rush. The radio edit is a monster, will take a while.*

Back to the session. Layering the final chorus, muting a synth line that didn't land. I cross-checked Bishop's hook against current chart-toppers. She'd be mad if I filtered her too commercial, but it was my job to make her sound like herself, only more.

Time passed. I turned on the neon under the shelves, ate a protein bar without tasting it.

When I finished the last cut, I uploaded it to the label's drive. Email all business—no typos, every bullet point addressed.

I sat back, cracked my knuckles, looked around the studio. Four years solo, and now I missed her like I'd never learned how to survive without the noise she brought.

My phone vibrated again.

> *just wrapped. dying. if I don't see u I'm gonna riot.*

I hesitated, thumb hovering. Every "yes" to Bishop was a lottery ticket, wasn't it? It could win, could be a dud, could cost more than I had to give.

I typed:

> *I'll come over.*

Sent it before I could think.

She didn't reply right away. I re-read the last message. Somewhere in the last twenty-four hours I'd lost the ability to sound like I didn't need her.

In the emptiness of the studio, I was stalling. Didn't want to get up and get into that car. Wondering if wanting her this much was the same thing as setting myself up to be gutted all over again.

Love that skips the wound is just ghostwriting, no more and no less. And you for damn sure can't hold a boundary while someone's deep inside you. I knew that. She knew that, too.

We had to talk.

The Conversation I've Been Avoiding Since Track One

Bishop

SHE WAS ALREADY LATE.

I'd tried not to watch the clock, but every five minutes I'd circle the

175

kitchen, pretend to look for a snack, and end up at the window. The city outside was black, gray, and yellow, streetlights fuzzing the air with a fake halo that made everything look cinematic. My phone was face-up on the counter. No new texts. I scrolled my timeline just to see if she was ghosting in real time, like maybe she'd post a "Just dropped the hottest stems" humblebrag while leaving me to rot in my own anticipation.

I imagined her coming up the stairs, every step measured, her brain already running through every possible outcome before her fist even touched the door. I tried to picture what she'd say, how she'd stand, but every scenario ended in my humiliation, so I stopped.

Instead, I did what I always did in moments of acute dread: I started making up verses.

By the time she rang, I'd drafted a hook in my head and a dirty little bridge I'd never get away with on the radio. I opened the door mid-line and there she was, hoodie zipped all the way up, hands buried in her pockets. She looked tired, and beautiful, and a little dangerous, the way a room sounds right before the monitors blow: full, and warm, and too much.

"Hey you," I said, aiming for easy, and reached for her face.

She let me kiss her, soft and clean, but her hand landed on my chest, palm firm enough to be a stop sign. She leaned back just far enough that our foreheads didn't touch.

God, we were a mess. After last night, I'd hoped we could skip right to the part where we just kept touching each other, never needing to talk. Maybe go to sleep, wake up, and start all over again. But Shiloh's energy said she'd spent all day rehearsing a conversation instead.

"We need to talk," she said.

The words snapped me so hard I almost laughed. I mean, come on. You go to Bishop's house for three reasons, and a "talk" was at best the amuse-bouche.

I tried to keep it casual. "Damn, was it that bad? I can do better, promise."

She didn't smile.

I'd spent years in green rooms, prepping for interviews where the next question could either crown you or drag you through the tabloid mud. You could always spot the moment before it happened—the micro-glint in the interviewer's eye, the slight lean forward, the way the air would pull taut as a string about to snap. Shiloh was leaning in now, but not toward me. She was bracing herself against the furniture of my ego.

"I promised I'd come back," she said, voice steady in a way that made my stomach drop. "I'm here. Being here with you feels good. Maybe a little too good. But I can't just pretend the last four years didn't happen."

The joke rose in my throat before I could stop it. Something about ruining the vibe, about how we were doing so *good* this morning. Couldn't we just have *us* back for a day before blowing it up again?

"I'm serious, E." Her eyes locked on mine, no escape route. "I need you to be serious too."

The joke died. My hands didn't know what to do, so I shoved them in my pockets, then pulled them out again, settled for crossing my arms. The apartment felt like it was shrinking, walls pressing in.

"Okay," I said. My voice came out shakier than I wanted. "Serious. I can do serious." I swallowed, forcing a crooked smile. "But—I mean, I haven't seen you since this morning. Like, what, ten whole hours? I'm basically experiencing Shiloh withdrawal. It's a medical condition. Do we have to do this right now?"

Shiloh's expression didn't change. "Yes. We do. If we don't, we're just going to keep doing what we did last night without talking about this."

The firmness in her voice killed any other deflection I might've tried. No room to negotiate, no opening to charm my way into postponing this. She wasn't angry. That might've been easier. She was just...resolute. Like she'd made a decision in that studio and nothing I said was going to change her mind.

Shiloh's not someone you sweep off her feet. Never has been. Shiloh is someone you *ask*. Come the fuck correct, or don't.

"Okay," I said again, quieter this time. The smile dropped. "Okay."

She didn't sit. Neither did I. We just stood there, five feet of hardwood and four years of damage between us.

"Why didn't you fight for me when the label said no?"

The question hit like a fist to the solar plexus. I opened my mouth. Closed it. Tried again.

"They kept saying the magic was in me. That you made me sound good, but they could get me better producers." My voice cracked. "You had options. Your family's studio, connections. I had one shot and I—" I stopped. "I took it."

Silence.

I was talking too fast, filling the silence with explanations that sounded hollow even to me. Shiloh just watched, waiting.

"And I thought—I mean, everyone was saying we were too close, too dependent on each other creatively, and maybe they were right? Maybe we needed to branch out and—"

"Is that what you wanted too?" Her voice was gentle. Not letting me off the hook.

The question stopped me cold. My hands twisted in my shirt hem.

"I thought it would be good for both of us," I said, hearing how hollow it sounded even as the words left my mouth. "Everyone kept saying we were drowning each other. That I couldn't be Bishop if I was still just—" my hands said what I was struggling to get out. "—half of us. And I fucking believed them."

"I didn't say that."

"No." I looked at the floor, at the scuff marks on the hardwood, at anything but her face. "You didn't."

The silence stretched. The fridge hummed in the kitchen, the muffled bass from someone's car passing outside. My hands twisted the my shirt again.

"I was terrified," I said finally. Felt like pulling glass out of my throat. "Of how much I—" I stopped. Restarted. "You. I needed you. For the music and for—*fuck*—for everything else too. And I couldn't take you this time. I didn't know how to tell you."

I risked a glance up. Her face was carefully blank, that producer mask she wore when she was listening to a bad take and trying not to show it.

"You could have called," she said, quiet but devastating. "You could have explained. Instead, you just...disappeared."

"I know."

"That's not an answer, Bishop."

"E," I corrected automatically, then winced. "I'm a coward, okay? I'm a fucking coward about this shit. Every day that passed made it harder. How do you—" My voice cracked. I swallowed hard, forced it steady. "How do you apologize for something that big?"

"You didn't get to make that choice for me. Had me up here wondering if I had done something to make you leave. It hurt!"

The words stung like a slap. She was right. Of course she was right.

"I told myself a clean break was kinder," I said. "That staying in touch would just make it worse. But really, I was just..." I waved my hands helplessly. "I was ashamed. And the shame turned into silence and the silence turned into years and I don't know, Shi. I don't have a good answer. I just fucked up."

Everyone says choose career over love when you're young. Great advice. Real helpful. Doesn't mention what the fuck you're supposed to do with the love part once you've already lost them.

She was quiet for a long moment. "I need to know about Skye."

My whole body locked up.

"Wait—did Cam say something to you?" The question came out sharper than I meant it. "At lunch? Because Skye knows I don't fuck with Cam like that. If she's running her mouth to Cam about us—"

"E—"

"And then *Cam's* in your ear about it?" My pulse thumped in my throat, heat creeping up my neck. "That's wild. That's actually fucking wild."

"Nobody said anything to me," Shiloh cut in, firm. "Cam made one comment at the mixer—'Tell Skye I said what's up.' That's it. I'm asking *you* about Skye because I need to know where we stand."

I forced myself to stop, to breathe. My hands needed something to do. I shoved them in my pockets.

"What about her?"

"Are you still sleeping with her?"

"No." The answer came fast, defensive. "We weren't together when—"

"That's not what I asked."

I moved away from her, pacing toward the window, then back. Needed the movement or I was going to crawl right out of my skin.

"I haven't talked to her since before we—" I gestured between us. "It was just physical. An arrangement. No feelings."

"There's no easy way for me to ask this. But I gotta. When did you get tested last?"

The question was so Shiloh—direct, practical, no judgment in her tone. Just information she needed.

I stopped pacing. "Two months ago. Negative. I can get re-tested if you want."

She nodded, something in her shoulders relaxing slightly. "Okay."

"We were careful," I added, not sure why I felt the need to explain. "Always. That was one of the rules."

Shiloh was quiet. Processing. Then her eyes found mine again, and I knew we weren't done.

"I need her to know it's over," Shiloh said, still standing in the same spot, immovable. "Completely."

"I'll end it." The words came easier than I expected. "I mean—shit, in my head it was already over the second I kissed you. Maybe before that.

Maybe the whole time." I swallowed. "But I'll make it official. I'll tell her."

"I need to know it's just us." Her voice was firm, no room for interpretation. "I can't do this halfway. Not again."

Something in my chest cracked open. She was setting ground rules. Which meant she was planning to work it out. With me.

I stopped pacing, turned to face her fully.

"Look, I've—" My hands were doing something stupid in the air. I shoved them back in my pockets. "I've tried. With other people. I tried to want them the way I—"

Fuck. Start over.

"You know how you get with a mix, right? And you're EQing and you're compressing and you're trying to make it hit, but something's just...off? And you keep tweaking it, but it never sounds right because the fundamental frequency isn't there?"

I could feel myself doing it—turning it into a metaphor, making it about music instead of about us—but I couldn't stop because the direct thing was too big and too true and I didn't know how to—

"That's what it was like. Every single person after you. The frequency was wrong."

My voice broke on the last word. God, I hated that. Hated how my throat was doing that thing where it gets tight and your words come out smaller than you meant them to.

"I kept thinking about you. The way you'd—" I laughed, but it came out wrong, too wet. "The way you'd alphabetize your plugins. Who the fuck alphabetizes plugins, Shiloh? And you'd get so hyped about some compressor algorithm that I didn't even understand, but I'd just sit there and watch you explain it because—"

I had to stop. Breathe. Try again.

"It's you, Shiloh. It's just—it's only ever been you. And I know that sounds like a line, I know I'm good at lines, but I don't know how else to say it. I've been with people and I kept wishing they were you. Wishing they'd tell me to stop talking so much. Wishing they'd fix my shit without asking. Wishing they'd—"

My hands came up again, helpless, still moving. Shiloh caught them. Held them still between us.

"I don't want anyone else. Not like this. Not ever like this."

Something shifted in her expression. Not softening exactly but acknowledging. Like she heard me, even if she wasn't ready to fully believe it yet.

"How do I know you won't run again?"

There it was. The core question. The one I didn't have a perfect answer for.

I could've lied. Could've manufactured something that sounded good, promising, certain. But Shiloh would see through it. She always did.

"I tried to make music without you. I tried to be happy without you. It sucked. The music sucked, I sucked. I don't know how to be a person if I can't be honest about that. I tried to reach out. Two years ago." I kept going, words spilling out in a rush, until my eyes burned because I needed her to really hear me. "I know—look, I'm not trying to make it better or whatever, I just need you to know I tried. I called. Texted. You blocked me, which—yeah, obviously you did, I earned that, but I was spiraling and I just—"

I stopped, forced myself to slow down. Failed.

"That's when I got the tattoo. The lyrics. Our lyrics." My hands wouldn't stop moving, gesturing at nothing. "It was stupid. Melodramatic as hell. Very on-brand for me. But I needed you to know I didn't just—it wasn't easy, Shi. Staying gone. I tried to come back, and you were already done with me. I didn't try hard enough. I know I deserved it. It still hurt real bad."

Shiloh sniffled.

Fuck. *Fuck*. I did that. I made her cry and I hated it and I couldn't take it back.

She was so still I worried I'd broken her.

Finally, she said, "You could've just told me that."

"I'm telling you now."

"Little late," she said, but her voice had lost its edge.

I stood, moved to her side. Close but not touching. "I want this if you do. Even if it's messy as fuck. Even if it's hard."

She nodded again. "That's all I need to hear."

My throat felt raw. "I can't promise I'll be perfect. I fuck-up. I panic. But I'd rather try and fail than not try at all."

She moved to the end of the couch, sat down but kept space between us. The distance felt intentional, necessary.

"I want to try, too. We go slow." She nodded. Not a question. "We talk about things instead of avoiding them. If something scares you, you tell me. You don't just disappear on me again. I swear to God, E—"

"Okay."

"And we finish the album first. Prove we can work together before we try to be together."

That one hurt. I wanted to argue, to say we could do both, that keeping them separate was impossible when everything about us had always been mixed up together. But I'd lost the right to argue when I walked away.

"Okay," I said again. Sat down and tried like hell to not rub my face with relief. "Slow. Talking. I can do that."

The lie sat on my tongue. I wasn't sure I could do any of it. But I'd try. For her, I'd try.

Silence settled between us, heavy but not hostile. More like the pause between tracks, waiting to see what came next.

"Can I..." I started. Everything felt too big right now. Too much space between us. "Can I still hold you? Or is that breaking the 'taking it slow' rule?"

Shiloh considered, her face unreadable. "I don't want to need you," she said quietly. "Spent a long time getting over that."

The words hit like a fist. "Yeah. I know."

"But I do." Her voice cracked. "I fucking hate it, but I do."

I reached for her hand, held it tight. "Then hate it. Be pissed about it. Just—don't hide it from me."

She searched my face.

"You're asking me to stop waiting for you to leave." Her voice was rough and worn down.

"Yeah." I squeezed her hand. "I am."

She looked at our hands. "I don't know how to do that yet."

"I know. I'll wait."

Then she shifted closer on the couch, closing the distance I'd been too scared to cross.

I wrapped my arms around her, careful, like she might vanish if I held too tight. She settled against me, head tucked under my chin, and for the first time all night I could breathe properly.

I was allowed to touch her again.

"I'm sorry," I whispered into her hair. "For all of it."

"I know." Her voice was quiet but steady. "We'll figure it out."

We sat like that for a good minute. The neon from the store across the street came in through my window, painting the walls in bands: blue, red, then blue again. The colors kept changing but we didn't move.

This wasn't a happy ending. Not even an ending, really. Just the start of something fragile and awkward and new. All that hope I'd been carrying alone, gone. Replaced by something harder. Honesty. That's all we had now.

After a while, Shiloh looked up at me. Eyes red, lashes clumped to-gether. She managed a small, crooked smile, then leaned in and kissed me. Soft. Lingering. Nothing hungry about it, just steady. A promise that maybe, this time, neither of us would run.

Slow

Shiloh

ONE MONTH LATER, AND Bishop still hadn't finished "Cathedral."

I printed the tracking schedule anyway—session at three, final vocal takes for the centerpiece track, the one the label actually cared about. The one Bishop kept finding reasons to delay.

Jinx showed up right on schedule, hauling his gear in with the efficiency of someone who'd done this a thousand times. Within minutes, the vocal chain was up: vintage U47, Avalon preamps, the outboard LA-2A Bishop always wanted.

When Bishop arrived exactly on time, Jinx did a visible double-take. "New world record. You early for a court date or something?"

She ignored him, eyes finding mine. "Don't want to get yelled at by

Ellis, do I?"

The subtext wasn't subtle. Jinx missed it entirely and went back to prepping the DAW.

Bishop moved to the booth without ceremony, grabbed her headphones, positioned herself at the mic. Through the glass, she looked at me. Ready?

I flicked the talkback. "You want a warm-up or just go for take one?"

"Take one," she said. "Always take one."

The track kicked in—glitched-out synth-bass and a chopped gospel sample. She rapped the first verse clean, only two breaths out of place. I marked takes, flagged sections for punch-ins, kept my face neutral even though her delivery was making my chest tight.

"First two bars are tight," I said over talkback. "But you dragged the end of the second verse."

She grinned. "I like it that way."

"I know. Do it my way once, then we'll see."

Four more takes. Every one different. At one point she caught my eye and switched up her phrasing just to see if I'd notice.

I did. Of course I did.

Watched her through the glass as she reset for another take. Bishop, who performed chaos for the world, who never let anyone think they had control—here, in my booth, she gave it up. Trusted my ear, my direction. Waited for me to tell her when she'd nailed it.

It did something to me, seeing her like this.

Jinx set up for punch-ins. We stacked the vocals. By noon, we had a comp track that made my arms prickle. Jinx patched it down, did a rough mix, and pushed play through the mains.

The chorus slammed. Bishop's voice soared, then broke on the very last word—deliberate, perfect. For a second, nobody moved.

"Holy shit," Jinx said. "That's the one."

Through the glass, Bishop grinned at me. Not the show grin. The real one, half-cocked.

I killed the mains and saved the file, trying to ignore the way my pulse kicked up.

The second block of the session went smoother, mostly because I refused to look at her unless I absolutely had to. I busied myself with the comp tracks, scrubbing the same four bars until my brain turned the vowels to mush. If Bishop noticed, she didn't say anything—just floated between the kitchenette and the couch, scrolling her phone or muttering into her notes app, writing and rewriting the bridge I'd pushed her to finish.

Jinx got sucked into the wiring closet for a solid thirty minutes, chasing a phantom buzz in the monitor chain. The moment the door swung shut, the control room was suddenly too quiet, all the little noises amplified: the click of my mouse, the tap of Bishop's nails on her phone, the faint hiss of static from the speakers.

She drifted over to the console, leaned against it, arms folded. I pretended not to notice, but my body clocked every inch she got closer.

"Show me the take you liked," she said, voice pitched low for just us.

I slid over, cueing up take three. She bent over the desk, close enough to see the blue paint flecks on the monitor bezel, close enough that I could count the individual lashes framing her eyes. I hit play, then soloed her vocal stem. The room filled with her voice, stripped bare of backing, every catch and break laid open.

She listened with absolute focus, brow furrowing at the tiny imperfections, the almost-cracks that she'd left in on purpose. When it hit the line she'd stumbled on, she cocked her head at me.

"You kept that?"

"It sounded real."

She chewed her lip, then nodded. "Okay. Play it again."

I did. This time she followed the waveform with her finger, tracing the peaks and valleys, every so often her pinkie bumped my hand on the fader. I forced myself to keep my hands steady, to focus on the screen, not on the way her scent—spice and sugar, like the cereal aisle at midnight—settled in the air.

The track ended. We both sat, unmoving, for a second longer than necessary.

"I'm gonna comp the end with the backup from take four," I said, voice tight.

"Do it," she said, not moving away.

She watched me as I worked. When I started to explain the logic of the compression chain—why I'd set her attack at 40 milliseconds, why I layered a second limiter under the main—I reached for the mouse at the same time she did. Our hands touched, just briefly, skin on skin.

The effect was instant. My hand jerked back, but hers stayed put, warm and solid on the mouse, almost provoking me to try again.

The air went thin. Her gaze settled on me, saw in my periphery the way her lips twitched at the corner. Four weeks since I'd kissed that mouth. Four weeks of showing up to work like nothing had changed.

"Careful, Ellis," she said, voice dropping lower. "Thought we were taking it slow."

I pulled my hands into my lap. "We are."

"Just checking." She still hadn't moved her hand. " 'Cause you look like you wanna jump me every time I breathe."

I went hot from collarbone to forehead. "I'm literally just trying to make a good record," I said, which would've been more convincing if my voice didn't crack on the last word.

She laughed, low and delighted. "Whatever you say, boss."

I stared at the monitor, refusing to look at her. "I need to bounce these stems and check the EQ on your BGVs."

She let the silence hang, then said, "You're cute when you panic."

I was about to fire back when she reached out and took my wrist, gentle but certain. I turned, startled, and she pulled me toward her—slow, like she was giving me every opportunity to say no.

I couldn't. Needed something at that moment, just to take the edge off. From the looks of it, she did, too.

She kissed me, thorough and unhurried. There was no audience, no performance, just the press of her mouth against mine, the world narrowing to this. Her other hand came up, fingers cool on my jaw, tilting my face just so. I forgot how to breathe. Forgot everything except the taste of her and the way she hummed approval into my mouth, like she'd been waiting hours for this.

When she broke away, I was dizzy. She grinned, but her eyes were soft.

"Back to work," she said, stroking my cheek before slipping away.

The door to the wiring closet banged open. Jinx stomped back in, oblivious, a spool of patch cable over one shoulder. "Think I got it sorted," he said, plugging in a test line. "Hey, can we roll another take, or is Bishop on vocal rest?"

I cleared my throat, scrambled for professionalism. "She's up. We'll punch in from the bridge."

Bishop didn't even look fazed. She grabbed her headphones and walked back into the booth like nothing happened.

We ran another three takes, all better than the morning set. There was a rawness now, a ragged energy that made the track feel alive. Even Jinx noticed. "That's fucking nuts," he said after the last one. "You good, B?"

"Never better," she said, then winked at me through the glass.

The afternoon blurred: session files, bounced tracks, emails to the label, tech notes for Jinx to double-check. By six, the main session was done, only cleanup left.

Jinx shut down the gear, humming Bishop's hook under his breath. "You want me to send these out tonight, or wait till you two are done fiddling?"

Bishop's eyes bugged out a little.

"Send the rough," I said, quickly. "I'll do the final edit after dinner."

He saluted, then packed up, oblivious as ever. "Catch you tomorrow, Bishop."

"Don't party too hard, Jinx," she said. "Wouldn't want you hungover for my next Grammy."

He laughed, shaking his head, and disappeared down the hall.

The moment the outer door closed, the studio fell silent. Just me and Bishop, surrounded by a thousand tiny lights and the faint scent of lavender and sweat.

She stretched, then leaned back against the console, watching me. Her hand went to the chain at her collarbone—just for a second, thumb catching the links—then dropped.

I pretended to organize my notes, but mostly just fumbled with loose sheets and re-capped my pen six times. My heart was already doing something stupid.

Bishop's eyes drifted toward the couch. Stopped. Snapped back to me.

I looked down at my notes. Very interesting notes. Suddenly fascinating.

Neither of us moved.

Finally, she said, "You gonna stand there all night, or are you gonna ask me to dinner?"

My heart flipped. Oh. "Dinner?"

She shrugged. "Or drinks. Or coffee. Or we could just sit here and stare at each other until one of us dies."

I tried to play it cool, but my mouth did the smiling for me. "Dinner."

"Cool," she said, grabbing her jacket. "I'm starving. You driving, or am I?"

"We'll take my car," I said, already halfway to the door.

She caught my wrist again as I passed, this time just a squeeze, then let go.

The quiet between us wasn't awkward anymore. It felt like potential—like the first rest in a song, just before the downbeat.

I locked the studio, and we stepped out together into the evening.

Bishop was jittery, which should have been my first clue. The way her hand kept going to her chain, twisting it, then dropping to her phone, then back to the chain again. I'd seen her play a thousand sold-out rooms, walk into label meetings with a smile that could peel paint off the walls, get a tattoo with less hesitation than most people had ordering lunch.

We got in my car, a sensible hatchback that smelled faintly of car freshener and fabric softener. She fiddled with the AC vents, adjusted her seat, opened the window down an inch and then up again. At the first stoplight she said, "It's not a date, by the way."

Her knee was bouncing the way it used to when she had too much in her head. I knew what I would have done before. I kept my hands on the wheel and my eyes on the road.

"Obviously. We're just two co-workers eating food so we don't die. In close proximity to each other."

"Exactly," she said, but the relief in her voice was too strong to hide. "Just wanted to make sure we were on the same page."

I wanted to tell her she didn't have to try so hard. That we could just let it be what it was. But then I remembered how she'd looked at me through the glass, how she'd kissed me in the control room, and I realized I was just as down bad.

The Trini spot was off a side street in Echo Park, squeezed between a strip mall pharmacy and a vape shop. The kind of place you could walk by a hundred times and never notice, unless you were specifically looking for it. Inside, the tables were a hodgepodge of mismatched wood and Formica, chairs rescued from different decades. The walls were the same yellow as the curry, spattered with band stickers and Christmas lights that blinked even in the middle of summer. The air was humid, packed with the smell of allspice, cilantro, and oil hot enough to burn the hair off your arms. Smelled like my grandma's old place when she was still alive.

"You again," the waitress said as she pulled up to our table.

"You know I can't stay away," Bishop said. "Doubles and a side of tomato choka, please. Make it extra spicy." She gestured at me. "And make sure it's good—don't want to get clowned for being a punk."

The woman barked a laugh and scribbled a note. I ducked my head, not sure if I was supposed to be embarrassed or proud.

"And for you, sir?"

"Curry chicken roti," I said, my voice low but still unmistakably feminine.

The server blinked, caught herself, and her smile twitched wider, just a beat too late. I was used to it. People clocked the short hair, the button-down, the way I sat—assumed one thing until I opened my mouth and the vowels gave me away. She scribbled down my order, eyes darting back once, maybe to double-check.

We were seated as far away from the window as possible, elbows nearly touching. Bishop relaxed a little, sinking into the seat, long legs sprawled out under the table. She flicked through the laminated menu even though she'd already ordered, then handed it to me with a theatrical flourish.

"Pick a drink. There's three choices and all are good."

The food came out fast. Doubles heaped with chickpeas and pepper sauce, a plate of tomato choka, two giant buss-up-shut rotis with my chicken. The smell hit first, then the heat, then the salt. I ditched the plastic fork. Nobody eats this food with utensils if they know what they're doing. Bishop was already tearing into the food, chickpeas tumbling back onto her plate as she folded it up with her fingers. I grabbed a piece of the buss-up-shut and scooped curry chicken, the roti soft and warm in my hand. God, it smelled like home.

The choka was hot enough to make my eyes water, the bread soft and greasy in the best possible way. I chewed, swallowed, blinked away the tears. Grandma would suck her teeth at me for being a wimp about the heat, but this was absolutely perfect.

Bishop watched me, waiting.

I took another bite, then another. "Okay. You're right. It's good."

She beamed, pleased. "See? Still slaps, even out here. But it hits different when you're not home."

For a while, we just ate, passing plates back and forth, mopping up every trace of sauce. Conversation was easy. Lighter than it ever was in the studio. I told her about the assistant engineer who'd set fire to a patch cable, about the time I'd been locked in a vocal booth by accident for two hours. She told me about her worst-ever festival gig, when the headliner got caught fucking the promoter's wife and the entire backstage turned into a hostage situation.

"I didn't even get paid," she said, licking choka from her thumb. "But at least I got a good story out of it."

I laughed my ass off, and she looked at me like she'd just solved a puzzle. For a second, I felt like the version of myself I forgot about—the one who used to talk too loud and laugh until my ribs hurt—was still in there somewhere.

The plates were empty, the table a mess of napkins and paper plates. I sipped my Ting and watched as Bishop dragged the last of the buss-up through the sauce and popped it in her mouth.

She glanced at me, then looked down, almost shy. "Can I tell you something?"

"Sure."

"You made me want more. And I wanted to be the person who could give you that, I swear I did. But I couldn't—I didn't know how to keep that promise. So I left before you could watch me fuck it up."

I didn't how to hold that. My hands felt too big, too awkward. So I reached for hers, palm up, offering.

She took it. Her hand was warm and she didn't let go.

We sat like that, palms touching on the table, as the restaurant emptied around us.

After a while, Bishop nudged my foot under the table. We were getting too sappy, too past *us*. "So. Over-under on how many tracks Cam's got about Romi Dulce this time? I'm saying five, minimum. Girl's got more Romi bars than Romi's got wigs."

I snorted. "Three, tops. And anyway, apparently, they did that performance and nobody ended up bald. It kinda looked like—like they were, y'know. Enjoying it too much."

Bishop's eyes went wide, her hand clutching her chest in mock horror. "Modern diplomacy in action. I need to see this. You and me having dinner, them not throwing heels at each other on stage. Next, you're going to tell me Quill and Dev posted up together at a cigar lounge. World peace is possible."

I choked on my Ting, caught between a laugh and a cough, and Bishop grinned, all satisfaction. For a second, it felt like we were just us again—no pressure, no history, just the kind of stupid industry gossip that always made her funnier than the rest of the world.

The check came. I reached for it, but Bishop was faster, sliding her card to the server with a practiced flick.

"I got it," she said.

"I can pay, you know."

She leaned in, voice conspiratorial. "Let me have this. I owe you about four years' worth of dinners."

I let her win. It was easier than arguing, and it made her smile.

We stepped out into the night, air cooler now, the city humming in the background. The walk to my car was half a block away, but neither of us was in a hurry.

At the car, I unlocked the door, but we didn't get in.

"I had fun," I said, because I couldn't ask her for more.

"Me too," she said.

We stood there, suspended, not ready to break the spell.

Finally, Bishop leaned in, rested her forehead against mine. "You don't have to drive me if you don't want to. I can Uber back to the studio, make this easier on both of us."

"I'd rather take you home," I said. Almost said, fuck the album tonight, come upstairs and fold me up. "I know we can't. But I do."

Her voice dropped. "I want that too. Kiss you slow, take off your clothes, touch you everywhere, really slow. Take our time."

I whimpered.

"But first, we take this slow. No rush. Remember?"

She smiled, then kissed me. Nothing urgent about it. Just warmth, and her mouth, and the strange quiet of not waiting for something to go wrong.

Bishop peacocks. I anchor.

Except she was anchoring me now. And I didn't even have to ask.

The city spun around us. The future could wait. For once, I didn't want to be anywhere else.

Want Is A Knife, And I'm Bleeding

Bishop

I TRIED TO SLEEP. I really did.

First attempt: I lay on my back in the chaos of my bed, body humming like an amp left on standby. The sheets were the expensive kind, imported and pointless, because tonight the only thing they touched was my sweat and the ghost of her mouth.

I replayed dinner like it was a leaked demo—unmixed, no edits, raw and a little embarrassing. The way I'd watched her hands as she ate, the curve of her wrist lifting the plastic cup, the way her mouth looked when she licked curry off her lip. Shiloh laughed, and my brain saved the file under "best sounds." We'd spent years with only the clatter of studio gear and tense, professional silence. Tonight, there'd been actual laughter, even if it was just us and some lady at the counter. Afterward, when she reached for my hand, our palms stayed pressed together so long I forgot to breathe. Even the goodbye felt different—like neither of us wanted to let go, just hover at the edge and taste what we could, greedy for more.

My body didn't get the memo about "taking it slow." I still felt where she'd touched me, every synapse holding on for dear life. I couldn't turn it off, no matter how hard I tried.

Plan B: I fished my phone off the nightstand, hoping for a distraction. The screen flashed the time—1:19 a.m.—and a pathetic lineup of notifications. Some muted group text from Jinx (meme dump, three replies from a burner number that was probably Skye). The rest was all promo spam and a single, pitiful email from my own manager:

URGENT—Tomorrow's call is at 10 sharp, NO excuses.

I tapped through the day's stories, pretended to care about anyone else's highlight reel. A photo of Shiloh and Cam at lunch—she looked clinical and a little tired, but the light in her eyes said she was alive again. I zoomed in, greedy, like maybe I could see evidence of me on her skin, a hickey or a fingerprint, something to prove to Cam we'd happened.

The gummies wore off and we were tracking tomorrow. Didn't want Shiloh glaring at me from the control room because I forgot words, so here I was, trying to be still enough to drift.

I dropped the phone on my chest and let my head roll to the side. The apartment was dark except for the spill of streetlights through the blinds. Shadows pooled in the corners—open suitcases, two abandoned ring lights, a coffee table covered in old vinyl sleeves. I liked the clutter. It was proof of life, a record of the last seven days when I hadn't just dissolved in my bed, feeling sorry for myself. But right now, all it did was remind me how alone I was.

I closed my eyes. Tried to think about anything other than the taste of Shiloh's mouth or how her hands felt inside me.

That lasted eight minutes.

By 1:28, I'd given up all pretense. Licked my fingers. My hand slid down, under the waistband of my boxers, and I let myself feel everything I'd been holding back all night. The ache was almost a sickness, a tension that ran from the back of my skull straight down to the pit of my stomach.

I started slow, teasing myself, imagining it was her touch, not mine—how she'd kissed my neck, how her tongue darted out to test me, the deliberate way she'd unbuttoned my jeans back in the studio. I remembered how she'd looked at me, all focus and hunger, and my body tensed up, pleasure mixing with something sharp and desperate.

It only made me want her more.

Switched focus. I thought about the time we'd learned we liked making out with each other and couldn't stop, both of us drunk on each other and the idea of "need you right now."

I thought about that first time we figured it out. We'd gone to the store all brave, came home with a small army of rainbow dicks we barely looked at. I'd forgotten about them the second she got close. I remembered her hands on me, my mouth on her, the sounds she made when I was inside her. Both of us clinging like we were trying to merge into one person. Too desperate to need anything but our hands and mouths on each other. Sweating. Shaking. Perfect. That was the real thing.

I squeezed my eyes shut and came with a grunt.

After, I lay there tangled in sheets that felt like they were trying to strangle me, chest doing that fucked-up thing where it gets tighter instead of looser. Should've helped. Didn't. Just turned the wanting into something I could name now because I'd gone and outlined it in neon. Every nerve ending lit up and buzzing, waiting for the one person who could flip the switch. Ground the current. Make it stop humming.

My phone buzzed against my ribs and it felt like—What? One of those texts that changes shit and you know it before you even look?

I wiped my hand on the sheet, unlocked the screen. 1:49 a.m. This time, the text was from Skye.

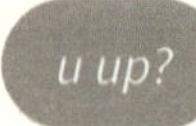

It was the classic "fuck me through your feelings *and* the mattress" invite, right on schedule. I read it twice. She'd never needed to add context before. The message was always the same: her place or mine, and you're not getting breakfast.

I rolled to my side, phone still in my hand, staring at the blue light like it might give me a sign. For a second, the idea of saying fuck it and letting Skye come over was almost enough. She was easy. Predictable. She just wanted me to fold her up. Gave zero fucks if I ghosted her for a week or forgot her birthday or ate all her snacks. There were no strings. No vulnerability. No risk.

But that was the problem, wasn't it? I didn't want easy. I wanted the person who could actually break me. Fucking away my feelings didn't hit the same anymore.

I set the phone down. The seconds ticked by. Stared at the spinning fan on my ceiling, the flicker of police lights three blocks away, the soft sound of a car alarm I'd stopped hearing ages ago.

The apartment was quiet, but inside, I was a mess.

Eventually, I picked up the phone and tapped out a reply.

can't. working it out with Shi. stay safe

I stared at it for a long time, then hit send before I could change my mind. Skye responded with a simple thumbs-up emoji, nothing else.

I exhaled. It felt like losing and winning at the same time.

I lay there, heart doing that thing, body wrong and still wanting—wanting to scream or smash something or just show up at Shiloh's door at 3 a.m. like a fucking disaster. Knock until she answered. Beg if I had to. Instead, I pulled the pillow over my face and tried to breathe through it.

This was it, then. Night after night of this shit, wanting her until I learned how to do it right. However many it took. I'd mark them off like a sentence I deserved. Let the need hollow me out if that's what it cost to not fuck this up again.

Tomorrow was another session. We'd be in the studio together. Alone.

I closed my eyes and tried to sleep, even as my body started to crave her all over again.

I woke up before my alarm even had the chance, body wired and dead at the same time, like I'd been electrocuted and left to cool. Sleep? Fifty minutes if I was generous, if you pieced together all the little moments I went under before my brain dragged me back. Spent the rest turning over lyrics that were too honest, filling up my notes app with shit I'd never say to her face.

Songwriting when I was this raw always meant my worst work or my best. No in-between. Last night it felt like both—first, an avalanche of lines about hunger and restraint, then a weird second wind where every verse was about how much it sucked to be good when all you wanted was to fuck up and fuck up bad. I wrote through sunrise, the keys of my old MIDI controller damp from the heat and my palm sweat.

I didn't even bother reading them back. I left the phone on the counter and let the words rot, figuring the truth would shake out in the booth, like it always did.

Shower. Cold. Soap that smelled like a botanical garden on fire. Manman called while I was picking out socks.

"I saw the article," she said. "You and Shiloh. Working together again."

Shit. Manman knew Shiloh. Fed her. Loved her. This wasn't like telling Skye to kick rocks. If I said it out loud, it became real.

"It's just the album, Manman."

"Mm-hmm." She kissed her teeth. "She looks good. You look happy."

"It's a photo."

"Mwen konnen pitit fi mwen an." A beat. "Be careful with her, bébé."

I didn't know what to say to that, so I said nothing. She let it slide, told me to eat something, and hung up with a "love you, bébé" like always.

Clothes: basketball jersey, loose cargoes, chain heavy enough to be felt but not seen on camera. I spent way too long picking out socks, landed on Adidas. Immediately picked out a matching pair of kicks from the shoe closet, because mixing was so tacky even I wouldn't do it. I ate half a protein bar, made terrible espresso in the machine I hated, and then left the rest of the apartment in a state that would make my cleaning lady leave passive-aggressive texts for days.

The drive to the studio was annoying. Went fast until the cars in front of me slowed. I barely noticed the streets, the stoplights, the panhandlers, people selling chopped fruit and flowers, joggers or billboard for my own face (NEW DROP, Cathedral, ALL PLATFORMS) with the date. Instead, I spent the whole ride rehearsing what I was going to say if Shiloh decided to bring up the thing I'd texted her last night. Or, worse, if she didn't bring it up at all.

The studio was already open when I got there. Shiloh's car was in the back lot. The inside was cool and dry. I shut the door behind me and, for once, didn't have a joke ready. She was already at the board, hunched over the laptop, headphones around her neck and a legal pad full of color-coded highlights next to her elbow.

She looked up when I came in, and the tired smile on her face almost made me turn back around.

"Morning," she said, voice a little hoarse.

"Morning," I echoed. I dropped my bag and tried to decide if I was supposed to hug her, dap her up, or keep a careful five-foot buffer. She solved it by doing none of the above. Just watched me, face calm, then looked back at her laptop.

"We're doing 'Tongues' first. You ready?"

I flinched, caught off-guard. "I thought we were holding that one till—"

"No," she said, and there was something deliberate in how she didn't look at me. "If we're going to do it, let's do it."

I nodded, throat dry. "Okay."

She tapped the mic on, waved me into the booth. I didn't bother with warm-ups. My voice was tired today but that felt *right* for this track.

The first verse was easy. Talk my shit, throw a little venom, let the flow trip over itself in a way that felt reckless but actually took five months of demoing to get just right. Metaphors stacked on metaphors—speaking in tongues, divine intervention, you used to translate me—the kind of wordplay that sounded like it was about one thing but anyone who'd ever had my mouth on them would know better.

Then came the hook. The part I was supposed to *sing*, not rap. The part where the beat drops out and it's just me and this confession disguised as a flex:

"You taught me a language I can't speak anymore/Now every word tastes like—"

My tongue tripped over the words so bad I almost laughed.

I heard Shiloh through the monitor—not the talkback, just her quiet exhale as she hit stop.

"Again, from the hook," she said. No commentary, no shade.

I did it again, this time with more edge, letting the break stay instead of smoothing it. When I finished, I heard a little "mm" of approval through the glass. It did something weird to my pulse.

"Bridge?"

She cued it up. This time, the backing was just synths and a ticking hi-hat, nothing to hide behind. I took a second to breathe, then went in. The words I'd written overnight bled into the bridge—more desperate, more honest than the demo version. I almost stopped myself, but Shiloh was watching, and it felt like the only real option was to lay it all out and let her hear it.

When I finished, she didn't say anything for a minute. Just ran the take back, head tilted, listening with the same face she made when she was about to dissect every flaw.

I left the booth. She had the vocal stem soloed and was running it back at 0.15 speed, so my voice sounded slowed all the way down, almost like a stranger's.

She pointed at the waveform, then at a spot near the end of the bridge. "That line—'rather drown than breathe without you'—did you change that on the fly?"

I shrugged, embarrassed. "Didn't mean to. Sorry."

"Don't apologize." Her eyes went wide. "That part right there is gonna end up in BookFizzr edits. Fucking brilliant!" She clicked the mouse, set a marker. "Do you want to try it again clean, or do you want to keep this?"

I looked at her, really looked, and saw the tired edge in her eyes—the way she kept checking her watch, the faint twitch in her jaw every time she thought I wasn't looking.

"Keep it," I said. "We can always comp in later, right?"

"Right." She made a note on the pad, then stood up, stretching her arms overhead, back cracking audibly. For a split second, her shirt rode up. Just enough to show a flash of skin above her waistband. I looked away, heat ticking up my neck, annoyed at myself for noticing.

When I glanced back, she was watching me. Busted. Her eyes held mine for half a beat, one brow raised, smirk playing at her mouth. The air between us went tight. Then she snapped back to business.

"Next up: 'Invasive Species.' Then we double the BGVs on 'Burial Plot.' "

I nodded, unable to keep from grinning a little. "You know, your session planning is getting pretty sadistic."

"Only way to get results," she said, and this time the smile stuck.

The rest of the session went in a blur. We worked through three more takes, my voice getting rougher and my brain turning to soup. Every so often, she'd stop and ask me to repeat a phrase, and I'd catch the micro-lift in her brow, the way her lips pressed together like she was holding something in.

At one point, I coughed hard enough to see stars. She paused the take, came in with a bottle of warm water, and handed it to me without a word. Her fingers brushed mine, barely, but it sent a shock up my arm.

She must've felt it too. For a half second we froze, close enough to see each other's pores, her hand still wrapped around the neck of the water bottle, my thumb grazing her wrist. Her eyes got real wide.

I opened my mouth to say something dumb, but she stepped back, shook her head. "Break time," she said. "You'll blow your voice if we don't."

We sat on opposite sides of the couch in the control room, water between us, not touching. My whole body ached. I wanted to make a move, bring her closer just to feel her body heat, but I heard the warning siren in my head: Don't push. Don't fuck it up. Her in my lap never ended with us fully clothed.

My arm ended up on the back of the couch without me deciding to put it there. Just resting. Not reaching. Except it kind of was reaching, wasn't it?

I could pull it back. Should pull it back. Left it there instead, suspended between casual and wanting. The gap between us felt geological. Continental drift in real time. And here I was, arm stretched across it, pretending it meant nothing.

Then I felt it. The lightest brush of fingertips against mine. So tentative I almost thought I'd imagined it. Shiloh's hand, reaching back without looking at me, her fingers finding mine in that thoughtful way she did everything.

I didn't think. Just responded. Threaded our fingers together, loose enough that she could pull away if she wanted.

She didn't pull away. So I kept it safe.

"What's the schedule look like tomorrow?" I asked.

She glanced at her planner, then pulled away to adjust her glasses. "Chelsea wants a finished comp for 'Cathedral' by Friday. She's threatening to bring in outside writers if we're behind."

I made a face at the loss of touch. "She says that every time and never means it. Like I'm going to let some Fizzr troll ghostwrite my shit."

"Just repeating what she said," Shiloh replied. Her voice was tight, but there was something gentle in the way she looked at me—like she wanted to say more but didn't know if it was allowed.

I tried again. "You sleep at all last night?"

She didn't answer. Not directly. Just shook her head, then started stacking loose sheets of lyrics into a neat pile. I watched her hands, watched the way her fingers moved, precise and delicate, and felt myself getting lost.

"You're staring," she said, not looking up.

I smirked. "Maybe I just missed your face."

She did look up then. Sighed. Same steady eyes, dark and unreadable, same calm that always made me feel like I was the one unraveling. Her face was leaner than I remembered, or maybe I was just paying attention in a way I hadn't been allowed to before. The close-cropped hair left her expression exposed, nowhere for her to hide—and she never did anyway.

But then she cleared her throat, back to business. "Can you do another hour? Or are you tapped out?"

"I can go all night," I said, then immediately regretted the double entendre. She snorted, shook her head, and went to set the mic up for the next take.

We didn't touch again, not even by accident. But every time she spoke into the talkback, I felt it in my chest—like her voice was the only sound in the world, and everything else was just static.

The final hour was always the hardest. My voice was just this side of raspy; my back ached from sitting, and every other part of me was raw from wanting. But this was what I lived for: the moment when all the bullshit and the endless retakes vanished, and the only thing left was the track you'd bleed out to if anyone asked.

We started with creative collab for a demo I'd laid down at three in the morning on my laptop—just a throwaway verse, really, but when I rapped it into the mic, Shiloh sat up straight and stopped marking up her session notes.

"Again," she said. "Do it exactly the same."

So I did. Twice. I wanted to keep going, but Shiloh flicked the talkback and said, "We have it," like there was no question.

We listened back on the big monitors. The room was silent except for the buzz of the lights and the words I'd just put down, running over and over.

"Want do pushups in my chest, blade talkin' slick/Taught myself patience, now the seconds bite back when I blink/It's a pit with a tongue, it keep sayin' my name when I fall/Built a cell out her cadence, still warm when the guilt start to crawl"

The hook came in softer than I expected—just a whisper, really, layered under the top line like a secret. It was the most honest I'd ever been on record, and it scared the shit out of me.

When the last beat faded, neither of us moved. I stared at the console, trying to act cool, but my fingers twitched.

Shiloh was the first to speak.

"That's it," she said. "That's the album. That's the thing that's going to make people lose their shit."

I swallowed, couldn't talk, just nodded.

She played it again, volume low. This time I watched her face instead of the waveforms—how her jaw tensed on my favorite lines, how her eyelids fluttered closed during the chorus. I couldn't read what she was thinking right then.

The phone rang, slicing through the spell. Shiloh flinched and answered before I could stop her.

"Ellis," she said, back in business mode. A beat passed. "No, we're still working. Yes, I have the comp. Yes, it's better than the demo. No, you can't hear it until Friday. Because it's not done, Chelsea. Two weeks is barely enough."

She caught my eye and did the universal hand sign for "kill me." I grinned, finally able to breathe.

"Yep," she said, "we'll see you then." She hung up and slumped back in her chair. "Two weeks. She's already emailing the press about the single."

I laughed. "Gonna leak it herself if you don't."

"She would," Shiloh agreed. Then, softer, "We can do it. I know we can."

The studio felt small, suddenly. Holding too much air inside our chests.

"I should get home," I said. "If I don't, I'll sleep on the couch and wake up with back spasms."

She nodded but didn't move. "Right."

I gathered my bag, unplugged my phone, double-checked that I hadn't left a trail of snack wrappers or empty seltzer cans behind. Her eyes tracked my every movement.

At the door, I turned back, wanting to say something epic or romantic, but all I could manage was, "Two more weeks."

Shiloh smiled, tired but real. "Two more weeks."

I left before I could fuck it up with another joke. Or do something stupid, like kiss her. Wouldn't be able to stop there.

In two more weeks, we wouldn't have to stop ourselves anymore. I could wait.

Forty-Six Minutes

Shiloh

THE STUDIO WAS DEAD silent at two in the morning, but the lights stayed up for me: soft orange along the floorboards, blue under the racks, rainbow ping-ponging across the channel meters. With the door sealed, all the outside sound was filtered out—no street noise, not even the low thump of subwoofers. Just the nervous tick of the wall clock, the hum of equipment, and the faint static in my left ear from twelve hours of headphones.

I hadn't left the chair in hours. The coffee in my mug was cold, skin on top like a bad latte, but I didn't want to get up to move it. My laptop was sandwiched between two racks of analog gear, monitors splayed in an arc that made it look like mission control for a space program.

The to-do list on my phone glared from the center of the desk, digital ink crossed through half a dozen bullet points: bounce all stems, verify 48kHz master, label each print with initials for legal, review metadata, review again, fix Bishop's last-minute lyric note ('bitch' can't air on radio, mark for edit). I'd printed and signed three separate versions of the mixdown summary and triple-checked the publishing paperwork, as if the labels' lawyers could sense blood in the water.

I stopped, flexed my hands, and rubbed my eyes hard enough to see red bursts. The skin under my glasses ached from where I'd pressed the frames into my cheekbones. Every time I closed my eyes, I heard the reverb tail from track four, the tiniest click in Bishop's overdub that I knew only I would hear. My body felt like one long, unspooling headache.

On a normal night, Bishop would've been here, perched on the corner of the couch with her knees up, phone in one hand and a bag of Chicago-mix popcorn in the other, tossing out ideas faster than I could catch them. But now it was just me and the circuits, her voice living inside the files like a ghost.

I ran my tongue along my teeth, tasted the sharp edge of old coffee, and scrolled to the bottom of the document. There was a line from Bishop, buried in the comment thread from a week ago:

> *If u disappear into ur bat cave for more than 2 days I'm sending a wellness check. Or an ex-orcist. Don't make me embarrass u in public, Ellis.*

She'd meant it as a joke, but the warning landed anyway. I hadn't slept more than an hour or two at a stretch, and every time I thought about taking a break, I saw her face—urgent, hopeful, a little afraid that this album wouldn't fix what she needed it to fix. If I fucked up, she'd have to live with it. I was the last link in the chain, and I felt every pound on my neck.

Above that comment was another one from three days earlier. Just a photo attachment, no caption. Her test results, all negative. She hadn't made a production of it, hadn't asked for praise or turned it into a bit. Just sent it and moved on. I'd stared at that image for a full minute before typing back a single heart emoji. The first one I'd ever sent her.

She'd replied with:

> *iconic. im framing this.*

I cracked my spine, rolled my head, and reached for the bottle of ibuprofen. Two down the hatch, chased with a slug of water. Then back to the screen.

I'd just started rechecking the cross-fades on the stems when the email landed, bolded and urgent at the top of the inbox.

Subject: FINAL PRE-MASTER: Bishop - Cathedral

My thumb hesitated over the touchpad. This was it. The last chance to call an audible before the album left my hands forever.

I sat back, wiped my palm on my thigh, and queued up the download. The file bar crawled across the screen with excruciating slowness, the studio Wi-Fi somehow slower at 2 a.m. than it was when six people were streaming anime next door.

I closed my eyes while I waited. Rubbed my temples. Tried to summon up the feeling of that first week in the studio—before the deadlines, before the label started breathing down our necks, before the past bled into every word we wrote.

I started at the top of the playlist, thumb poised on the space bar like it might bite me if I hesitated. When the first track bloomed in my ears, I made myself sit perfectly still—no multitasking, no screens, no taking notes. Just let it run.

The opening orchestral synth glided in, exactly as I'd shaped it, a slow build that held back until the pressure was almost unbearable. I caught myself tapping the pad of my index finger against my thigh. On the first downbeat, Bishop's voice came in: cold, clear, then edged with the distortion we'd spent days arguing about. I'd dialed it down, afraid she'd hate it, but in the headphones it sounded tight. Just how an album should hit when you press play.

Track four was "Cathedral." She'd recorded the final in one take, voice already raspy from a morning spent yelling at her agent over a blown contract. The verses were tight, measured, but the last chorus she'd gone all-in and her voice rasped on the final line. In the session, I'd marked the spot—possible comp, clean version available—but I never swapped it out. The break made the song, made her sound human. Even if it cost her a note on the radio edit.

At the moment of the rasp, my pulse jumped. I winced, then smiled. She was going to kill me when she heard it.

Track five was a blur of chopped samples and verse that didn't bother pretending to be about anything but sex and betrayal. Bishop said she had written it at 3 a.m. after a fight, drunk and mean. It was the track that nearly ended the album; she and the producer fought so loud the session runner texted later to ask if she was okay. Now, the song was perfect, every line angry and precise, every ad-lib a gut punch.

I played the album through, a forty-six minute sprint with no pause. By the end, my limbs were numb, my jaw so tight it ached. My face felt hot and tight. I realized my face was wet only when I reached up to adjust the headphones and my fingers came back slick.

I let the silence ride for a long time. No one to see me, no one to ask what I was thinking. In the emptiness, the sense of accomplishment was massive, terrifying. We'd done it. I'd done it. The album was better than the one Bishop had tried to make without me—deeper, more honest, riskier. Not a single track for the algorithm but built to trend. It was real in a way nothing in the last four years had been.

I didn't move for five minutes, maybe more. I thought of that Police song: every gesture, every sound, pure magic. My dad used to play it on repeat. Now I understood why.

Then I picked up my phone and set it on the desk, screen up. A single text notification waited:

is it done?

I stared at it, heartbeat going wild. I didn't answer, not at first. I wiped my eyes on my sleeve and read it three more times, like the words might change.

Then I typed, simple and flat:

> *It's done.*

Bishop's reply was instant:

> *can I come over*

I hesitated. My place was twenty minutes away. Bishop's, ten in the other direction. There was only one right answer, and it wasn't about the music.

> *Studio or my place?*

Her typing bubble flickered in and out.

> *wherever u are*

I set the phone down, tried to breathe. The studio was still dark, monitors cycling through their power-save colors, the memory of Bishop's voice vibrating in the air. I turned the volume down, rolled my chair back, and waited for the knock on the door that would mean this wasn't all a dream.

A half hour later, she arrived. She texted once from the parking lot—*here*—and then I heard her sneakers down the stairs and the rustle of bags.

She knocked, three rapid taps, and when I let her in the air changed instantly: a shock of her cologne, the crinkle of the takeout bag, her presence filling every square foot like feedback. She wore a hood up, chain gleaming in the half-light. Her eyes had dark circles like she'd run a marathon with her own anxiety.

"Hey," she said. For the first time since we started doing this again, her voice sounded small.

I cleared my throat. "Hey."

She didn't look at the gear, or the screens, or even at me. She walked to the kitchenette, dumped the takeout on the counter, and then just stood with her back to the room, breathing in and out. Her hands fluttered a little as she wrestled with the plastic utensils, then gave up and leaned on the counter, head bowed.

I didn't know what to do with my hands. I wiped them on my jeans, then folded them in my lap, then finally stood and approached the counter, keeping a careful two-foot distance.

She turned, finally, and met my eyes. Her mouth worked around the next words like they were heavy.

"How are you?" she said.

It knocked me off balance. I'd expected the bravado, the jokes, the instant, relentless banter. But she was just looking at me with concern.

"I don't know," I said, honest. "It's a weird feeling. Usually there's something left to do."

She nodded, slow. "Yeah."

I glanced at the bag. "You brought food."

She shrugged, but her eyes flicked over me, sharp. "I figured you weren't taking care of yourself because you never eat when you're in the zone. Manman would fly down here on the next flight with a slipper ready if she knew I hadn't fed you." Her tone tried for casual, but I heard the care under it. "I can leave it if you're not..."

"No, I want—" I stopped myself from saying *please don't leave*. "Stay. Thank you."

She ducked her head and started unpacking: tacos wrapped in foil still warm, little plastic baggies of salsa—green, dark danger red, red—limes cut in quarters, chopped onions and cilantro in their own containers. She used my only real plate, arranging everything with a kind of reverence, then handed it to me with both hands.

We ate in silence. Every time I looked up, she was chewing slow, eyes fixed on a point just over my shoulder. She finished first, wiped her mouth, and then started to pace. The nervous energy was back, winding her tighter and tighter.

Finally, she stopped in front of the mixing desk, hands on the edge. "Can I hear it?"

I swallowed, my throat suddenly tight. "Yeah. Let me load it up."

She slid into the chair, spun once, then sat still with her hands folded.

I queued the file, loaded her preferred headphones, and handed them over. She took them, fingers brushing mine. For a second, we both froze.

She put on the headphones, closed her eyes, and pressed play.

For forty-six minutes, I watched her. She didn't move except for the smallest twitches in her mouth, the slow spread of her hands out on her thighs, the way she sucked in a breath at the start of every track. Toward the end, she started to cry—silent, just tears leaking down her cheeks, not even bothering to wipe them away. She listened to the end, took the headphones off, and set them down so gently I thought they'd break.

She didn't say anything for a good minute.

I reached over. Brushed my knuckles against her cheek, catching the tears. She leaned into the touch immediately, eyes closing, almost waiting for permission to fall apart. I let my hand linger there. Thumb tracing the edge of her cheek.

Then she opened her eyes. "You did it."

I shook my head. "We did."

She looked at me, unblinking, and for a second she was Evienne again. Brilliant, raw, and terrified. Her hand found mine, squeezed hard.

"Thank you," she said.

We sat like that, hand in hand, until the clock on the wall clicked over to 4 a.m.

She let go, wiped her face, and said, "What now?"

The question was so simple I almost laughed. I'd been dreading this moment—the end of the work, the start of whatever came next—but now that we were here it felt like the only thing that mattered.

I opened the email client, drafted the final note to the label. Attached the master, the alternate edits, the stem archive. At the bottom, I typed both our names in the credits. When I hovered over "send," I looked at her.

"You sure?" I asked.

She looked at the screen, then at me. "We almost didn't get this. Kept thinking we'd run out of time before we did." Her hand tightened in mine. "Send it before I say something else embarrassingly sappy."

I pressed send.

The whirr of the outbox was anticlimactic. For a second, it was just us and the quiet.

I stood. Crossed the space between us. She looked up at me, surprised, and I didn't let myself hesitate—just sat in her lap, facing her. Careful but sure. Wrapped my arms around her and pulled her close. Pressed my lips to her forehead, held them there.

"Proud of you," I said, quiet.

Her arms came around my waist immediately, tight. Like she'd been waiting for permission. "Proud of us." Her voice frayed just a little.

I meant it when I said it back. "Proud of us."

We stayed like that. Me in her lap, us holding each other. The finished album spinning somewhere in the cloud. The future waited just outside the door.

The 'I Could've Had Her' Speech (A Tragedy In One Act)

Bishop

THERE'S A PARTICULAR SHADE of nothing that happens after you finish an album. I was marinating in that flavor of nothing at every red light on Sunset, my truck idling like it wanted to take a nap right there in the intersection.

The label's last email was open on my phone: "We'll be in touch. Next steps forthcoming." Translation: put your life on hold, stress eat everything, don't call us, we'll call you.

I was wearing joggers and a tee, hair half-damp and hood up. On the passenger seat: empty Starbucks, old wristbands, protein bar wrappers. My brain was a lawnmower on high—whether the mix was too wet, whether anyone would even care in a week. And beneath that, the knowledge that the only person I wanted to talk to about it was Shiloh.

The light turned green. The Prius behind me laid on the horn, and I jerked forward on autopilot.

I thumbed out a message:

> *thanks again for being the goat. owe you big. let's eat something disgusting next week.*

Hit send.

The photoshoot building loomed up: glass-wrapped monstrosity with valet parking. I pulled into the lot and let the guy in the vest judge my car's interior. The elevator ride was dead silence except for faint sounds of chaos above.

The set was a hive: stylists, interns, bored models. They'd built a whole white-on-white vibe for the shoot. Someone had hung a printout of my face by the catering table.

I sat in a makeup chair while strangers worked on my face and hair. Neither asked what I wanted.

While they worked, I scrolled Shiloh's reply:

> *you're ridiculous. but same. congrats on surviving the deadline. wanna celebrate with trash food after your shoot? let me know.*

I tried not to smile, but it snuck out anyway.

The photographer wanted "rebirth," "vulnerability," "the new you." I stood in the glare thinking only of what I hadn't said.

They ran me through the poses—wounded angel, cathedral mode, hands on a white piano. Mid-shoot, someone asked about my vision for the album cover. I shrugged.

"Whatever makes my mom cuss me out."

When it was over, I stripped off the borrowed clothes and slipped out before anyone noticed.

I sat in my car, engine off, and stared at my phone. I scrolled to Shiloh's last message and tried to decide if I was brave enough to call.

My phone lit up with a FaceTime to Shiloh before I could chicken out.

She answered on the second ring as I fumbled to prop my phone against the dashboard mount. Her face filled the screen and my brain went static. Bronze skin catching the harsh conference room lighting, those thick dark frames she wears when she's been staring at a screen too long, curls framing her face in that effortless way that makes me want to write terrible poetry. Fuck.

"Hey," I said, trying to sound normal and not like I'd just forgotten how breathing works.

"Hey." She smiled. Small and tired sounding. "You survive the photo-shoot?"

"Barely." I shifted in my seat, angled the phone so she wasn't getting the full nostril experience. "They wanted me to look 'reborn' while standing on a white piano in this weird asymmetrical thing that was at least seventy-five percent vest, twenty-five percent shirt. Like, conceptually it was giving phoenix-from-the-ashes, but realistically I just looked confused and possibly concussed."

She laughed and leaned back in her chair. I watched the way her entire face softened when she was genuinely amused and not just being polite. "That tracks. Did they at least feed you?"

"Kale salad and sparkling water. I'm literally wasting away as we speak. This is my ghost. You're talking to my ghost right now."

"Tragic." Movement on her screen—someone walking past, papers shifting. She glanced off-camera, pushed her glasses up with one finger. When she looked back, I caught that little furrow between her eyebrows that means she's already mentally back in work mode but fighting it. "I've got about five minutes before they drag me back into another post-production meeting. How are you holding up?"

And there it was. Not "how was your day?" but "how are you?", now that we're done, now that the boundary's technically gone but we haven't—like, we haven't *talked* about it. I had the words ready. But saying them meant risking the fragile thing we'd just rebuilt. So I didn't push. Kept it light. Let her come to me on her own time.

I picked at the steering wheel, tried not to stare at her face like a creep. "I'm good. Weird. You know, the whole waiting thing. It's like, okay, bad metaphor incoming, it's like when you finish recording and you're just sitting there in the silence after and you don't know if what you made is brilliant or trash, you just know it's *done*, and that's terrifying?"

"Yeah." Her eyes dropped to something on the table in front of her—probably her hands, she does that when she's thinking—then back to the camera. Dark eyes behind those frames, looking right at me. Warmth crept up the back of my neck. Tried not to sigh. "It's weird on my end too. Finishing something and then just...sitting with it."

"You miss me yet?" I said it light, teasing, but I just knew my face was doing something extremely transparent.

She bit back a smile. I *saw* it, the corner of her mouth twitching, and suddenly there was no air in this parking garage. Long pause. "Maybe."

"*Maybe?!*" I grinned, probably looking completely ridiculous. "Ellis, you wound me. You're killing me. This is murder."

"You'll live." That smile finally broke through, and Jesus Christ, I need to get a grip. "What are you doing right now?"

"Sitting in a parking garage, FaceTiming you, having a whole crisis.

Living my best life. Very glamorous."

"Sounds thrilling." Maybe it was better that we weren't in the same room. One of us would find some reason to break the touch barrier, lock eyes and that's when clothes started coming off.

"It is, actually." I cleared my throat, tried to blink away *that* image. "So. Trash panda food. When?"

"Depends." She tilted her head, studying me through the screen. A curl caught the light. "Are you trying to ask me on a date, or are we still pretending this is just two colleagues celebrating a finished project?"

My brain short-circuited. Completely flatlined. She said it so casually, like she wasn't lobbing a grenade directly into my lap and then just—just *waiting* to see what I'd do with it.

"I—" I started, then stopped. Blinked. "What do you want it to be?"

"I asked you first."

"Shiloh."

"Evienne."

And there it was. My actual name. The one only Manman uses, and only when I'm in trouble or she's being sentimental. She'll be happy to know we're trying.

But hearing my name in Shiloh's voice, in that low deliberate way she has, man. My chest felt like someone turned up all the frequencies at once, everything suddenly too loud. I watched her looking directly at the camera, at *me*, totally calm like she didn't just reach past every defense I have.

I exhaled. Tried to find words that weren't just "yes please I've been dying here, please put me out of my misery."

"I want it to be a date," I said finally. "If that's cool with you."

The silence stretched just long enough to make me panic. She looked down, maybe at her hands, and when she looked back up, there was this softness in her eyes that knocked the breath clean out of me. "Yeah. That's cool with me."

I blew out a breath in relief. "Okay. Good. Cool. Very cool. When are you free?"

"I've got label stuff through tomorrow, then I'm starting prep for Cam's EP next week—"

"Right." The mention of Cam's project hit different, even though I'd known it was coming. Even though I'm happy for Shiloh. Even though it's not—it's fine. "Yeah, no, that's—whenever works."

"Wednesday?" She leaned forward slightly, and I could see more of her face now, the faint shadows under her eyes from too many late sessions. "I should be clear by then. Few days to breathe."

"Wednesday's perfect."

Someone appeared in frame behind her—just an arm reaching for the door. She glanced over her shoulder, sighed, and a few curls shifted with the movement, catching the light. I'm being extremely normal about all of this. "I have to go. They're waiting."

"Go. Make them pay you properly. Demand absurd amounts of money. Buy a yacht. Do it for the paparazzi pics."

"That's the plan." She paused, her eyes softened again. Shiloh bit her bottom lip for half a second before she spoke. "E?"

"Yeah?"

"It's nice talking to you. About things not related to work." She looked down, and I could see her doing that thing where she plays with the edge of whatever's in front of her notebook. Fighting a smile. "We should do more of this."

I smiled, stupid and wide and completely unable to play it cool. "Will do. Absolutely. Consider it done."

"See you Wednesday."

"Wednesday."

She waved—small, casual, devastating—and the call ended. I sat there staring at my blank screen like an idiot, grinning at my steering wheel, replaying the way she'd said my name, the way her curls had caught the light, the way she'd *smiled* at me.

A date. An actual date. No boundaries, no "let's finish the album first." Just us.

I'm so fucking screwed.

I started the car and pulled out of the garage, already mentally cataloging every trash food spot in LA.

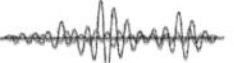

The party was in one of those pseudo-industrial lofts downtown, all exposed brick and pipes that led nowhere, strung with lights. The air stank of expensive booze, weed vape, and the desperation of people whose job was to make music happen, but who had made none themselves in years.

I wore my armor: faded designer jeans, a tee with SORRY I'M LATE stitched in rhinestones, a crushed velvet jacket the color of dried blood, and sneakers so white they could signal airplanes. Chains stacked at my throat, two diamond studs in my ear—none of them meaningful, but together they made a kind of statement: untouchable, post-ironic, above caring about the rules.

I walked in like I owned the place, because that was how you survived these rooms. Inside, people circled in predatory circles: producers and managers and pop starlets, all rehearsing their elevator pitches in real time. I smiled at the familiar faces, clapped backs, ducked handshakes in favor of elaborate dap-ups.

Every single person who hugged me whispered some version of, "Can't wait for the new record," as if the world was actually holding its breath. They asked when the next single would drop, what it would sound like, and who I'd worked with this time. I lied by omission or just redirected: "It's raw, it's weird, you're not ready." They lapped it up. It was all foreplay, no payoff. Nobody in this room cared about the actual music.

I checked my phone every five minutes, scrolling through nothing. I watched for Shiloh's name to pop up, even just as a notification. Eventually, I got one:

> *stuck in a meeting. label's being psycho about the credits. will hit you after.*

My chest went cold. I thumbed a reply:

> *survive the bloodbath. let me know if u want company later.*

No answer.

I needed a drink.

I shouldered my way to the bar, weaving past a crowd of kids who were all dressed like it was opposite day—three in neon sweats, one in a vintage fur, one in a mesh tank that showed off tattooed ribs and nothing else, which was wild. The bartender clocked me and slid a whiskey across before I said a word. I nodded in thanks.

From the corner, I spotted Cam Wolfe. She was posted up with an A&R suit, both of them laughing over something on her phone. Cam looked different offstage: hair cut in some weird pixie mohawk situation, silver bamboo hoops, dressed in a crisp white shirt unbuttoned at the throat and dark trousers with suspenders and chelsea boots. She caught me staring and winked.

I turned away, but not fast enough.

Two minutes later, Cam was at my elbow. She held a highball glass in one hand and pointed at my jacket with the other. "Love that," she said, voice smooth as aged bourbon. "You always could wear the hell out of a bad idea."

"Thanks," I said. "Didn't realize the clown convention let out early."

She barked a laugh, loud enough to turn heads. "You're funny, E. Always were."

We were both veterans at this. Banter, the careful circling, making everything sound like a joke so no one had to admit they were feeling anything real enough to make someone swing on them. She leaned in, eyes locked on mine. "So. You happy with it?"

"With what?"

"The album. Your life. The whole 'new you' thing. I hear it's got people in the building losing their shit."

I shrugged, sipped my drink, and made a face like it was too strong. "It's just music. They'll get over it."

"Not really what I asked," she said. "But cool. Stay mysterious."

She glanced back at the A&R suit, then at me. "You see Shiloh lately?"

The question punched a hole straight through my act.

I forced a smile. "Why, you miss her?"

Cam held my gaze. "I'm just saying, it'll be cool to get back in the studio with her again."

She meant it casual, just another project, but the word studio lodged somewhere deep in my chest. People didn't realize: that's where it always started for us. We were 'bros' playing PS4 and riding bikes until we caught each other staring over the mixing board and couldn't hold it anymore. I kept my face neutral, but inside, something old and fragile rattled.

What I didn't say: You're also doing that Cam thing, pretending you've never tried to get with Shiloh when we both know you did. I almost wanted to laugh—like we were all still teenagers, circling each other, acting like nobody saw the obvious.

"Fight someone? Nah, I'm a lover, baby. Specifically, a lover of leaving parties before they get weird." I flagged the bartender for another drink I didn't need. "Which this one already has."

Cam snorted. "Party's barely started and you're already plotting your escape route. Classic." She sipped her drink, let the silence dip for a beat. "But listen. You know I'm not after Shiloh, right?"

I froze. "I don't—"

"You did. You've always had one eye on me like I'm gonna steal her." Cam's tone was amused, not mean, but it still landed like a slap. "I'm not. Gave that up a *long* time ago. I just think it's funny watching you freak out."

"That's—"

"Payback? Yeah, a little. You slid into my situation with Skye. Now you know how it feels." Cam grinned, well, like a wolf. How fitting. "But honestly? Shiloh's already yours. She was *always* yours. Even when you left. That's the part that should terrify you—not me."

Cam downed the rest of her drink and slammed the glass down.

"Treat her good this time, or *else*."

And just walked away. No goodbye, no joke, just left me standing there with my armor clattering to the floor.

I stared at my hands, suddenly cold.

The party moved on around me. Beats thumped, people howled, and somewhere in the back a group started a loud, off-key karaoke session. But I couldn't hear it. All I heard was Cam's voice in my head, on repeat:

She's already yours. She was always yours. That should terrify you.

It did.

I got in the car and slammed the door harder than I needed to—like that would do anything, like the sound could reset my whole god-damn nervous system. Sat there gripping the wheel, staring at nothing through the windshield. Behind me, the party was still going—bass thumping through brick, someone screaming-laughing on the sidewalk. I should've felt better being out of there. I felt like shit.

Started the engine. Peeled out onto the street, headlights slicing through dark like I had somewhere important to be. Home was twenty minutes away. Twenty minutes of silence I didn't want, empty apartment waiting like a dare I wasn't ready to take. Turned the music up—some playlist I wasn't even listening to, just *noise*, something to drown out Cam's voice still rattling around in my skull.

Phone lit up on the passenger seat. Email notification.

Red light. I glanced down. Subject line: ALBUM APPROVED.

Read it twice. Three times. Body was basically nothing—one line, maybe two. "Moving forward with rollout. Great work, team." Like it wasn't the whole reason I'd been losing sleep for weeks.

Light turned green. I just—sat there. Stared at my phone like it might start making sense. Someone honked. I flipped them off without looking.

Pulled into a gas station, hands shaking, yanked out my phone. Typed without thinking:

> *hope the meeting wasn't a bloodbath. let me know if you want to trade war stories.*

Hit send before I could delete it.

Shiloh replied fast:

> *wasn't as bad as i thought. home now. you ok?*

I stared at the screen. Could've said no. Could've said, actually, Cam just annihilated me in three sentences and I'm about to vibrate out of my skin. Could've said, the album's approved and you're the only person I want to talk to. Could've said, I tried ten million different ways to tell you I liked you and I didn't want you to date Cam, I wanted you to date me and I'm not making that mistake again.

Instead:

> *just tired. you were right about the promo stuff, it's insane. hope you're sleeping. talk soon.*

Safe. Boring. A lie.

Her next text came a minute later:

> *i'm up. if you need me.*

My thumb hovered. Engine still running. Album approved. Shiloh awake. Me sitting in a gas station parking lot at midnight pretending any of this was fine, pretending I could just—What? Go home? Sleep?

Fuck that. Four years gone. I wasn't waiting another second.

Dots appeared. Disappeared. Appeared again.

> *Come over?*

I typed at the same time:

i don't want to wait anymore. can I see u?

The next text was her address.

I didn't even look at the road before I threw the car in drive. Didn't put the phone down, didn't think, just—turned around. Headed the opposite direction. Toward her place.

Homecoming

Shiloh

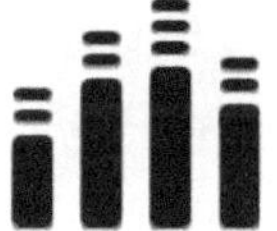

THE KNOCK WAS HARD enough to make me jump. Urgent raps. Not the neighbor, not a delivery. Not anyone except the only person who would ever knock like that.

I crossed to the door without checking the peephole. There was no reason to.

Bishop stood in the hallway in a ridiculous T-shirt and baggy jeans and blindingly white sneakers. Her hands balled into fists in her pockets. Her face was flushed, eyes wild and bright.

We stared at each other. Not a word.

The first time we'd been this close outside the studio, we'd spent a week at the basketball kids camp avoiding each other. I took the bottom bunk. Spent every night staring at the slats above me, hyper-aware she was right there. We made stupid jokes about everything except what was happening, us not looking at each other like "bros" anymore. The counselors thought we fell out with each other. That was fifteen years ago. This was worse.

Bishop sucked in a breath, chest rising and falling. "I couldn't wait until Wednesday," she said. The words were naked, no performance, no joke to hide behind. Just a fact, like gravity or terminal illness. "I know you're tired and it's late but—" She stopped, looking down, then back up at me. "I had to see you."

There were a thousand things I could've said. I said none of them. Instead, I stepped aside, pulled the door wider, and watched her walk in, every movement careful like the floor might vanish under her. She kicked off her sneakers.

Bishop was the one who broke the silence, always. She didn't even try to start slow. "I went to a party. Cam was there—whole thing sucked, she said some shit that made it worse, whatever—and then I'm driving home and I get the email. Album's approved. Like, officially happening. And I just—" Her hands sketched frantic shapes in the air, like she was still mixing the words, searching for the right stem. "I turned the car around. Didn't even make it to my place. Just...turned around and drove here."

I nodded, not trusting myself to say a word.

She laughed once, a tiny sound with no humor in it. "I spent too long telling myself I didn't miss you. I lied. I missed you so much I couldn't stand it." Her voice was shaking. "I don't know how to not want you, Shi."

I still didn't answer. I watched her hands, the way her thumbs worried the skin between her knuckles, the way her whole body vibrated with the effort of not coming apart.

"I know I'm supposed to be the chill one," she said, voice rough now, eyes wet. "But I care. I care so fucking much and I—I left home. I want to come back home."

I moved before she could try again. Crossed the three feet between us. She flinched. Bracing for the response where I pushed her away again. The one that started with *we should* and ended with her driving home alone.

I put my hands on her face. She was hot, skin feverish, breath coming quick. Her eyes went wide, searching mine.

"Kiss me."

Two words. Everything I had.

Her mouth opened. Nothing came out.

"I'm not saying it again." My voice cracked on the last word. Hated that. Didn't take it back. "So."

Her hands came up, shaking, and covered mine where they held her face. She was looking at me the way she had at Harmony Heights. Right before the first time, when we were kids and didn't know what we were starting.

Fuck it. I kissed her.

There was nothing gentle or slow about this. It was everything we'd shut down for months, years, all at once—like flipping a switch in a room full of gas. She made a sound against my mouth, and then she was kissing me back, hands clutching at my shirt, pulling me closer.

I tasted salt, sweat, the last ghosts of whiskey on her tongue. I felt the tremor in her jaw, the way her body went rigid, then melted all at once. We kissed like we were starving.

Finally, Bishop broke away, breathing hard. She pressed her forehead to mine. "Finally," she whispered, and I felt the word vibrate all the way to my spine.

Bishop's hands were everywhere—hot, frantic, starving for skin. She tried to push my shirt up, but I caught her wrists and held her back, palms tight around her pulse.

She froze, surprised. For a second we just stood, breath loud, faces close enough I saw the slight panic in her eyes. Her lips were parted, the lower one already swollen from our kiss.

"You promised me slow," I said. My voice didn't sound like mine. "Slow kissing, slow touching. Remember? I haven't been able to stop thinking about that."

I'd been going to bed with a toy that couldn't keep promises. Wanted the real thing, now.

The words hit her hard. She swallowed, then nodded, the movement jerky. "Yeah. Okay. Slow." Her voice was hoarse. Her hands trembled.

I let go of her wrists, but instead of backing off, I pulled her in, arms around her waist. I felt the shiver start at her ribs and roll all the way up. She went soft against me, like she'd let go of something she'd been clutching for years.

I kissed her again, softer, tracing the outline of her mouth with my tongue. She let me, eyes closed, her lips moving slow and deliberate against mine. I kissed the edge of her jaw, then her throat, my teeth grazing the skin just hard enough to mark her.

Bishop gasped, tilting her head back. "Shi—"

"Let me," I said, voice rough, hands sliding under her shirt. She was muscle and bone, every inch of her mapped from memory, but this was the first time I got to savor it. I lifted the shirt off her in one slow motion, knuckles grazing her ribs, and she raised her arms for me, obedient.

She was beautiful. She always had been, but now she looked like something sculpted. Her skin was dark, soft, stretched tight over lean muscle. I kissed the hollow of her collarbone, then lower, letting my mouth linger at the edge of her chest, kissed each new inch of skin, felt the goosebumps rise under my tongue. My fingers traced the tattoo that was still new to me.

Bishop's hands hovered at my waist, like she didn't trust herself to touch me without shattering the illusion.

I whispered, "bedroom," against her mouth.

She breathed out a low "yes." I was already dizzy from her, knees soft, pulse screaming at my throat. Then she steered us, hands gentle at my waist, walking me backward with her mouth on mine, step after step, like she'd practiced this in dreams and couldn't afford to fuck it up now.

Every time I tried to think, she kissed me again, deliberate, swallowing the words before they even formed. Heat from her skin. Pressure in the way her thigh slid between mine, slow and steady, the movement of someone who'd learned the value of patience and wanted to taste every second of it.

The hallway was a blur, just the drag of her hands on my arms, my shoulder bumping the wall. Once, I reached up and cupped her chin, thumb finding the pulse at the hinge. She sucked in a breath. Almost stopped walking.

Didn't.

Kept us moving. Kissing. The world got smaller, just the two of us, her scent everywhere, sweat and adrenaline and dark sugar. I heard myself gasping, desperate, didn't care. She grinned against my mouth, then went soft, hungry. No jokes. No brakes.

I hit the foot of the bed, knees bumping it, and she froze, forehead pressed to mine, both of us trembling with the effort not to fall. My glasses nearly slid off, but she caught them.

"Shi, can I take these off?" Her voice, lower than I'd ever heard it.

I nodded.

She set them on the nightstand gently.

The gesture shouldn't have been that hot. But watching her hands be so careful and deliberate made me throb. She was already undressing me without touching a stitch of my clothes. Already seeing me.

She looked at me and smiled, a twitch at her mouth, like she knew something I didn't. Hands on my hips, light at first, then firmer, fingers pressing into bone. Nobody ever told you how it felt to be wanted by someone who knew all your worst days, all your sharpest angles. She did. She knew every inch. Her hands said it.

Bishop pulled my shirt out of my waistband, slow enough to make it a threat. I raised my arms because what else was I supposed to do? Bishop peeled it over my head, deliberate, knuckles scraping my ribs, mouth already following the path she was carving out. No bra. No shame. I was exposed and she stared like she'd won something. Hard to say which one of us was more surprised.

She made a sound, low in her chest, just before she ducked to kiss the top of my shoulder. Warm mouth, soft scrape of her teeth, then down, lower, her tongue flicking over the line of my collarbone. Like she was sampling, not sure if she'd want to come back for seconds or eat the whole meal right here, right now.

I forgot how to breathe.

She kissed a line down my chest, mouth warm and sure, pausing just long enough to make my skin burn. Her knuckles grazed my nipple—casual, almost careless—until her lips closed over it and everything inside me spasmed. She circled it with her tongue, slow at first, then sucked, gentle turning relentless. Had the nerve to be humming while she did it. Sensation shot straight to my gut. I grabbed her shoulders, nails digging in without apology, needing her anchored. She didn't stop, just kept humming low, making me arch into her mouth, the rest of the world falling away until it was only her, only this.

She hooked her thumbs in my waistband and tugged, slow. Shorts, underwear, both in one motion. She knelt, all that height folding down smooth, and peeled them off like she was unwrapping a present she actually wanted. Bishop's hands on my thighs, mouth trailing after, slow on purpose, hotter when she took her time. I tugged at the belt on her jeans, pulling them over her hips, and Bishop kicked them off.

She looked up, face right there, dark eyes gone soft at the edges—not the look she gave the label, or the fans, or even the session runners. Just me. And she smiled, wide, all satisfaction.

You'd think that after all those years, I'd want to keep my poker face. But she had my number, always had. My stomach did a full nosedive, nerves and want crashing hard. If she noticed, she didn't say shit. Just kissed the inside of my knee, lips soft, and then higher, barely a pause, up to my hip.

She spent the next moments just exploring. Fingertips. Lips. Teeth, good God, one tiny nip and I nearly came off the bed. She hummed, low, mouth right on my skin, like she could taste my reaction. Which, fair. She always did.

She took her time. I mean really took it. One hand on my hip, holding me down, the other spreading my thighs just so. Wasn't shy about it, either. Bishop always said she liked the way I sounded and didn't care if the neighbors heard.

She pressed kisses everywhere but where I wanted her most, slow and mean, until I was breathing hard, flat on my back, legs open, everything on display.

"Slow enough for you?"

I let out a sound. Couldn't help it. Not her name, not anything. Just a sound.

She laughed, soft, and nipped the inside of my thigh, higher this time. Heat rolling in behind her mouth, every nerve underneath my skin sparking up.

"*Fuck*, you're soaked."

That's when she did it. Dragged her fingers down my slit, lazy as you please, in no rush to get anywhere. Touched me like she was checking the ripeness of a peach—thumbs circling just once, slow, seeing if the finish would scratch. Skin to skin, no filter, no shame, no hurry. The pads of her fingers mapped my knee, then the curve of my leg, all the way back up to where I was already slick and shaking. She didn't even act impressed. Just kept going, soft and slow, until my hips snapped up off the bed like they were spring-loaded.

She breathed out low and satisfied over my skin.

"This is malicious compliance," I groaned.

"Is it?" Bishop nipped at the inside of my thigh, then nipped its twin.

She licked her lips. Real casual. She didn't even need to look at me to know what she was doing to me or the sounds I was making.

"I need your mouth. Now."

"So bossy," she said, and ran her fingers down my slit.

What Bishop did to me couldn't be called mercy. She parted me with her thumbs, slow as honey, and then did exactly what she wanted, which was plant her tongue right on my clit and hover there. Not giving me an inch, just letting me taste the tension. If you ever want to know what the opposite of chill looks like, it's me with Bishop's face between my thighs.

She kept going slow, on purpose. Licked me exactly in the spots she'd mapped out with her hands. Nothing fast. Nothing even halfway generous. She worked me like I was the headliner and the rest of the lineup could go fuck themselves.

Bishop was not here for the radio edit. She tongued my clit in slow circles, no mercy, no commentary. She kept her hands on my thighs, holding me open, not tight but heavy enough that I wasn't going anywhere.

Both times I thought I was going to get there, she'd back off. She did it again. Backed off at the last second, like she was teasing a cat with a string. Classic. Could've made a drinking game out of it. Take a shot every time Bishop made me whine. Guaranteed blackout.

After the fourth time, she grinned up at me from between my thighs, smug as fuck, mouth slick, and said "not yet," before continuing her torture.

I glared at her, or tried to.

"Oh, you look *mad*," Bishop said. Tongue flicked, right at the edge, not even touching. "I'd say sorry, but you look kinda hot like this."

She was on some game show host shit. How bad do you want the prize? Say please, Shiloh.

I would've said her full government name if I could remember how to speak.

I dug my fingers into the back of her neck and dragged her in. Right where I needed her: mouth on me, hot and steady. She didn't move.

"*Please.*" I squirmed. The words rushed out, probably sounded desperate as fuck. "Let me come. I need to come."

You ever see a slow-motion replay of a championship hit? The kind where the air gets sucked out of the room, right before the impact? That's what she did to me. Licked me flat, then circled soft, and sucked just enough to make my knees weak. She wanted me loud. I gave her everything.

Bishop didn't back off this time, not even when I came. Just kept licking and sucking while my hips jerked—that guttural moan vibrating straight through my core. My body folded, undignified, hands scrabbling at her head like I was trying to hold on for dear life. Did I want her to stop? No. Did I want to do anything except ride it out, jaw slack, whole body gone rigid and useless and so fucking gone I couldn't hear myself choke out her name, three times in a row? Not really. Not when she was the only thing holding me together.

I made a sound, then went limp, like I'd been peeled apart for breakfast and left in the sun. Vision whited out. The only thing I saw was Bishop's face, smug and glistening like she'd just won the Nobel Prize and was already drafting her acceptance speech.

I reached for her. Didn't care that my body was still shaking. I needed her, right where I could touch her, none of this across-the-bed bullshit.

I wanted her close enough that when I reached for her, my hand didn't land on empty air. Bishop crawled up, eyes glazed, lips parted.

Her boxers were tangled at her hips. I hooked two fingers in the waistband, found the edge, and shoved down, not gentle. She made a desperate noise when I did it. Together, we got them off, then it was just me and her with nothing in the way.

I slid my hand between her legs. Wet. So fucking wet, her thighs were slick, too. Trembling.

"You got off on that, didn't you? Making me beg for it?"

"God, yes." Bishop's hips jerked when I touched her, and her breath went all sharp at the edges. I stroked her, slow, not even pretending to rush. If you'd put a mic on her heartbeat, it would have broken the needle.

She tried to play cool, but her head dropped forward and her hand landed on my shoulder, hard. She rocked herself into my palm, needy.

"Come on, lay back," I said.

She did. Bishop's head hit the pillow; her arms went up, biceps flexed, full-on surrender. The look on her face? Could've stopped traffic. She looked at me with her mouth open, eyes dark, skin shiny at the collarbones, breathing so loud I could've cued a track to it. All that hype about Bishop being the alpha? Right now, she was soft under my hands, just waiting.

I traced her inner thigh instead. Nails light, ghosting close but never there. Felt her clit throbbing, untouched, begging. Even as I trailed down her lips, each in turn, with my tongue.

Took my time. Let my tongue rest there, flat, just for fun. Make her wonder if I'd even remember what I was doing.

She looked like she could start a riot with her eyes, but her body was all anticipation. The tension, the hush right before the downbeat. I circled her clit, one slow circuit, then another, over and over again. No rush. Barely pressure. Just enough to make her feel it.

Bishop's hips jumped like I'd shocked her. Oh, she was ready.

I knew it. Watched her pulse hammer at her throat and her eyes slid shut like the sensation was too much, too soon, too easy. She could try to take it slow with me, but I knew what her body was saying before she did: now, right now, right now.

I leaned down and kissed her again between the lips on her face, wanted to feel it in her mouth the exact second I sank my fingers inside. I wanted the gasp. I wanted the give. I got both.

"Eyes on me," I said. Voice gone. Just sound and need. "Don't look away."

She tried. God, did she try. Her eyes fluttered, rolled, eyelids heavy, but I set my palm flat on her hip and pushed her back into the mattress, held her there so she couldn't run. This moment was hers. This was mine. Ours, again, finally.

I dragged my fingers out, slow, fucked them back in, the heel of my hand grinding her clit—slick suction kissing her with every thrust. Bishop's thighs trembled as her hips rose to meet me.

"Faster. So close." She gripped my forearm. I sped up, and her eyes squeezed shut with a full body tremor. "Fuck, Shi, you feel *so* good."

I crooked my fingers, and she broke, hard, gripping me, eyes locked on mine as I rocked against the spot again and again until she whined.

I didn't let go. Didn't blink. Didn't look away, not for one second. Kissed every moan from her mouth while she pulsed around my fingers.

When she finally dropped back to earth, I eased out, slow and careful. Her body went boneless, trembling, and then stilled. My hand was slick with her, the smell of her sweat and need thick enough to taste at the back of my throat.

Bishop was wrecked. No other word for it. She blinked up at me, biting parted lips.

I leaned in, found her mouth with mine. No rush now. Just the after-glow: softer, almost sweet, lips meeting in a slow roll, her tongue lazy and wanting and grateful. She tasted of salt, me, and whatever makes you hit send on a message you swore you'd never write.

She wrapped her arms around my neck and pulled, greedy, desperate to keep me close. I kissed her again. And again. The kind of kisses you give someone who just admitted to everything, who handed you the keys and said, here, take it all.

I touched her everywhere I could reach, letting my hands memorize her all over again. Not a single part of her flinched. Not a single part of me wanted to let her go.

We sprawled in the heat, mouths stuck together, sweat everywhere, the sheets already sideways on the bed. I didn't know where my skin stopped and hers started. Couldn't tell if the ache in my belly was hunger or relief.

Her tongue slid behind my teeth, slow, then hard and bruising, then slow. I tasted the years I'd spent pretending I didn't want her.

She drew her legs up, draping them over my thighs, guiding our mounds to grind together. I climbed on top and rocked my hips against hers. Wet and urgent, we rode each other hard, lost in the raw feel of skin on skin. Her hands clamped my hips then, locking that slick heat in place, pleasure flaring bright as I picked up speed, bucking faster into her. I gripped her thigh tight, chasing the building rush. Her nipple stiffened under my palm.

She looked down to watch the way our bodies joined with half-mast eyes, mouth open. We moaned low, grunted sharp as we came together, slick sounds filling the air. When we slowed, I leaned in. She sucked a bruise into my throat and marked it with her tongue, then kissed lower, jaw, collarbone, the quick bite over my tattoo. Her breath hitched when I touched the back of her neck to pull her closer.

You'd think we would've slowed it down, let the afterglow last. But we were too wound up to stop. We'd lost too much time already.

She said it into my ear, barely a sound. It hit somewhere so deep, I shivered. "Want to fuck you so bad. Let me?"

Easiest yes of my life. I nodded. Couldn't form a word.

The top drawer on my nightstand was a catalog of plans I never let myself have. I opened it, reached in, found what I needed, cool and familiar in my palm. The silicone, matte black, already buckled to the harness. No hesitation. I put it in her hands. Her eyes got real big when she realized how ready I was.

"*Damn*, Shi. You weren't playing around, huh? Had it locked and loaded already!"

I poked her with a toe. "Shut up."

She kissed me, then sat back on her knees and got to work, strapping the harness low on her hips. The shift in her body was immediate. A sharpness. The way her hands stilled, then steadied. With half-lidded, hungry yet focused eyes, she breathed through her nose as she looked at me and fastened it.

I watched her, spread out and waiting, skin slick, not even pretending to hide how bad I needed it.

She leaned over me, the toy heavy against my thigh, the heat of her body behind it. She kissed me again, bruising and rough.

"Tell me if it's too much," she said.

I arched up for her. Opened. Rubbed myself against the toy because the wanting was so sharp it hurt. Her eyes followed the motion and she groaned.

"Come *on*, E." Didn't recognize my own voice.

She lined up, pressed in. The stretch was obscene. Perfect. My body tried to chase her, tried to pull her in all at once and she gave it to me. All of it.

No easing in, no gentle lead-up, just the pressure of her hips and the stretch that forced every other thought out of my head. It was almost embarrassing how good it was. The way my body just opened to take her. I felt her everywhere—the grip of her hands on my hips, the heat of her breath against my neck, the way she filled me slow, then deeper, then so deep I couldn't even fake a poker face.

"You take it so good," she said, sliding out, and pushing back in. I arched up to meet her, nails scraping down her back.

I hissed.

You think you know yourself. That's the biggest joke. Because it turned out, I didn't know a damn thing about what I needed until I had her above me, breaking me open, giving me the full-damn-song, no edits, no fade-outs. I was obsessed with the sound of her skin slapping mine, the wet slide of her thrusts, the way she fucked me like she was angry and starving at the same time.

She lost the rhythm once and it made her curse under her breath. I liked that, too. I liked the fuckups, the honesty. When I bucked under her, she pinned me harder. I ground back fierce, pulling her deeper with my heels digging into her ass. Every time she bottomed out, I saw stars.

I said her name. Maybe not even the right way, but she caught it, made a fist in my hair, and gave me more. Bishop's other hand drifted to my face. Made me look at her, eyes glassy, sweat beading on her lip. No excuses, no escape hatch, either. My chest was heaving like I'd run a mile. I didn't even know what my face looked like. Probably ruined. Probably the same as hers, but with all the wiring on the outside and nothing holding it together.

She held my gaze and fucked me in slow, deliberate strokes, like she wanted to drive the point home, take out a billboard, maybe write a jingle about it. Shiloh Ellis, ruined on a Tuesday. I rolled my hips up into each one, matching her rhythm, breath ragged as I clutched her shoulders.

Her hand tipped my chin. Not sweet. Not cruel. Just real.

That's when she said it. Dropped it like a bomb nobody bothered to check for wires.

"I love you," she said, bottomed out inside me. "I fucking love you so much, Shi."

No warning. No lead-in. Just handed it over, naked, no wrapping. She didn't even flinch when she said it.

If there'd been a mirror in the room, I would have watched myself break. That's how fast it hit. The tears just happened, no dramatic build-up, running hot and stupid down my face. I made a sound, not even a word, just a gasp, like a mic shorting out mid-take.

She kissed my cheeks, my eyelids, every spot the tears landed. Said my name again, softer. Stayed with me, inside me, until I believed it. Wrapped my legs around her waist to keep her inside.

I tried to breathe, but the air was crowded. All the things I'd trained myself not to say pressed in my throat—that I needed her as much as I needed water, that wanting her was the ache in my beats, that there was no universe in which I ever stopped waiting for her to come home.

I said it how only she could hear. "You're mine."

"Yeah." She nodded. "I am."

She rested her forehead against mine, breath catching on something that wasn't air. Wet heat on my cheek that wasn't mine. I did not let her go. I held her face so she could see me.

"I love you too." It came out quiet. Certain. "Never stopped."

I said it again, just so she'd never forget that there was nowhere for us to hide from each other, anymore.

Her whole body tensed. Hips slowed. She kissed me again, hard. I wanted every second. I wanted it to last.

She thrust inside me like she'd lived there, all the years in exile nothing compared to this: body to body, heart to heart, breath to breath. The ache, the stretch, the way her hands held me like I was going to fall through the floor under her. Pressure steady, deep strokes pushing me higher. The air was all sweat and heat, sharp with the taste of her stuck to my lips.

She kept me together when I tensed. Kissed me through the tears. My eyes stayed open. Bishop fell apart, muscle trembling, mouth slick at the edges, the sweet ugly of her breathing as she lost it and hammered home until I gasped.

The moment hit, hard, a drop that blurred my vision, heat and pressure building. My hands clawed at her ass, urging her harder, faster. I'd never come that loud in my life. Didn't care.

She followed seconds after, hips grinding helplessly. Bishop shuddered against me, gasping "*Fuck,* Shi," into my throat. We collapsed. Sheets damp, legs all tangled up. Nothing left but the burn and the afterglow. The sound of her heart, wild under my palm.

She stayed inside until we both stopped shaking.

I held her there.

Eventually, she pulled out, careful, and I felt the loss of her like cold air. She rolled me on top of her, pulled me against her chest, arms wrapped tight around my back, my leg between hers.

We didn't speak. Just breathed together, syncing without meaning to, the way we always had in the studio. Instinct, memory, the physics of us.

Her fingers traced lazy patterns on my shoulder blade. My hand rested over her heart, feeling it slow from sprint to steady.

"Stay," I said finally. Quiet, but certain.

"Yeah." Her voice was rough. "Not going anywhere."

I believed her. For the first time in four years, I believed her completely.

As My
Person

Bishop

THE SUN IN SHILOH'S apartment hit different than anywhere else in LA. Big windows, west-facing, so every morning started bright as fuck, the light sneaking in at angles that made dust look like confetti. I never set an alarm anymore. My body knew to wake up the second the bedroom hit room temperature, which was about an hour before Shiloh. I'd roll out of her sheets—soft, nice, but never tucked in right—and pad barefoot into the kitchen, every other step catching on the runner she claimed was "impossible to vacuum."

This was the whole thing, now: coffee, arguments over whether oat milk is a war crime, and the sound of synth pads bleeding through her headphones from the "office" down the hall. If you'd told me a year ago

I'd want to be domesticated, I would've stared at you like you sprouted three heads. But I guess that's the joke, isn't it? Turns out, you can teach new tricks if the treats are good enough.

I made coffee every morning because Shiloh picked a machine where I only had to press a button. She could diagram a compressor chain blindfolded, but the Breville had too many buttons and she refused to read the manual.

The mug situation was a rotating cast. Today was the NERD 4 LYFE one, a Harmony Heights relic that neither of us had the heart to retire.

I sipped, burned my tongue, and leaned against the stove. From the hall, the sound of Shiloh's voice, low and quick, narrating mix notes for Cam's EP: "Needs tighter reverb, cut 2dB at 340, the panning in the second chorus is too surgical. Fix it."

She'd adapted her studio setup to fit into the spare bedroom, which was about as big as a nice hotel suite but with a better view. The wall behind her desk was a tangle of acoustic tiles and thumbtacked band flyers, next to shelves loaded with reference vinyl and poetry books. The air always smelled floral and of fresh cable insulation. I live here now, technically. My jacket was draped over a kitchen chair, my socks under the coffee table, my toothbrush in the holder next to hers. She had a dresser at my place, too. Sometimes it hit me sideways—how easy it was to move in, how nothing about this felt like a hostage situation.

Shi appeared in the doorway, headphones still on, blue pajama pants low on her hips, wearing one of my cutoff tees. She carried her own mug, the cool one with the brass knuckle handle, and set it next to mine.

I watched her work. She'd cradle the headphones with one hand, eyes flicking between the waveform on the screen and the notes on her tablet. Sometimes she'd mouth the words to the track, lips barely moving, and it was always a little mesmerizing. I used to think she was cold, but it's just that she focused so hard the rest of the world fell away. I loved that about her. I loved watching her do anything.

She caught me staring, smirked, and pointed at my mug. "You want to die today? You used six scoops."

I grinned, wide. "I like my heart rate high."

"You're going to liquefy your stomach lining."

"Isn't that the goal?"

She rolled her eyes, but not in a mean way. The edges were soft, almost fond. She sipped and grimaced, then nudged the mug back at me. "Straight battery acid."

The next half hour passed like every morning since the world stopped ending and started again: music, caffeine, the two of us in parallel orbit. I killed time by scrolling my socials, which was either vanity or research, depending on who you asked. People still cared, which was its own kind of weird. Every day, a new meme, a new DM, a new essay about "what Bishop's comeback means for queer music and the future of pop culture," usually written by someone who'd never even listened to my first album. Today, the chatter was about the tour dates leaking early.

I wasn't ready to think about it. Not yet.

I switched to Pixogram and went for nostalgia. Six months ago, our album release party. There was a shot someone caught—probably one of the label's photographers working the event. Shiloh was fixing my collar or my chain or something, being her usual particular self about details, and I was just...looking at her. Full attention, no performance, the kind of look that made it real loud I wasn't thinking about anyone else in that room.

I held out the phone, waggling it in her direction. "Fans are still ob-sessed with this one. Half of them think we're together, half think we're just 'close collaborators.' " I made air quotes with my free hand. "And then there's the horny contingent who saw this and decided they wanted us both. *So* many train emojis. It's actually impressive."

May y'all find someone who looks at you like Bishop looks at shi.ctrl, God bless, a commenter said.

She paused, took the phone, and inspected the photo with the focus she used on everything else. A small smile tugged at her mouth. "They can keep guessing too."

"You really like keeping people on their toes."

"I like that you're not hiding." She scrolled through a few more times, then gave up. "That's what matters."

I looked at the photo again—me staring at her like she'd invented sound itself, her hands on my collar, both of us in our element. My poker face was always trash. Especially when it came to her. "Yeah," I said. "I'm not."

She handed the phone back and returned to her desk, attention clicking back to her work in a heartbeat. "Let them speculate," she called over her shoulder. "It means they're not bored."

That was Shiloh all over: unbothered, unshakable, always two plays ahead. I watched her for a minute, the way her shoulders hunched when she was deep in a track, the way her foot tapped in time with the beat. I wanted to say something profound, like, "You know, I used to be terrified of what people thought about me." But I wasn't that person anymore. Now, I just wanted to be seen by her, not by the world.

I sipped my coffee, looked at the photo again. Six months ago, I would've sold an organ for the kind of peace I felt right now.

Maybe that was the secret. You stop performing and you get to be the real thing.

She caught me staring again. This time, she smiled—real, soft, and for me alone.

"Come here," she said.

I crossed the room and stood behind her, arms draped over her shoulders, chin resting on her head. She smelled like mint and conditioner and home.

She leaned into me, unguarded.

We'd been this way since the beginning, really. Junior year, I'd tried dating this girl. Cute, fat ass, into music, nose ring. Shiloh "butt-dialed" me halfway through our date. Called her back worried. She played it cool. Thirty minutes later: text about some vocal chain emergency. I bailed on nose-ring girl without a second thought, took the subway straight to the studio. No emergency. Shiloh was fine, everything was fine. I stayed till late anyway. Never called that chick back. Still don't remember her name either.

At the time I told myself it was about the work. But I knew—we both knew—I would've ditched anyone, anything, just to be in the same room as Shi. She'd called, and I came running. Simple as that.

This was still us, apparently.

Phone buzzed right then, killing whatever moment we'd been building. I wasn't really paying attention till this one, insistent and annoying as fuck. I grabbed it, read the subject line.

Tour schedule locked.

Fuck. My hands went clammy. Stared at it long enough for the words to blur. Everything shifted—not earthquake level, just a crack appearing in the foundation. Small. Getting bigger.

Put the phone face-down. Regretted it instantly because now I was staring at the blank back like maybe if I didn't see the screen, time would stop advancing.

Shiloh had her headphones on, but she clocked the second I stopped moving. Always waiting for something to go wrong. She pulled one ear off, looked at me. Eyebrow raised.

"You're vibrating," she said.

"Am I?" I tried to keep it light, but my voice was off by half a note.

She set her headphones on the desk, rotated in her chair, and fixed me with that producer stare, the one that brooked zero bullshit. "Talk to me."

I messed with a pen on her desk until realized I was just bullshitting. "Label wants me on the road for three months."

"How soon?"

"Six weeks."

She processed that. No surprise, no "wow." Just nodded, arms folding.

I kept talking, as if inertia would carry me through. "They want the full package: promo, live sets, press, radio, the works. No breaks."

"That's a lot," she said. Not judging, just math.

"Yeah."

The silence settled in. Not cold, just thick. My heart started to hammer, the urge to move clawing up my back.

"I haven't done a real tour since before all the..." I gestured. "You know. The you-and-me, then not-you-and-me, then implosion, then all the other fun stuff."

"You're nervous you'll flame out."

"I'm nervous I'll turn into the worst version of myself and not even notice."

She held my gaze. "You won't."

"You can't know that." I looked at the floor.

She stood and crossed the kitchen, pausing to top off her mug. Then she sat at the table, hands flat, waiting for me to join her. The invitation was clear. I sat. Tried to keep my legs from jittering under the table.

"You want to do it?" she asked.

I twisted the mug, thinking. "Parts of it, yeah. Not all the label-bait. I want to play for people who actually give a shit, not just industry creeps."

"Then do that."

"It's not that easy."

"Sure it is," she said, deadpan. "You say no to the rest."

I smiled, but it was weak. "You know they'll kill the whole thing if I start saying no."

She shrugged. "So?"

"So—I don't know. Maybe I need to prove I can actually finish something by myself for once."

She let that hang out. "You did. You finished the album."

"Yeah, with your help."

She snorted, low and amused. "E, you finished it because you wanted to. I just pushed the buttons."

"That's a pretty big deal."

She sipped, then set the mug down. "So, what's the actual problem?"

I hesitated. "I want you to come."

Her eyebrow shot up. "Come where? The tour?"

"Yeah."

She considered that, all logic. "I can't just drop Cam's project."

"I know. I'm not asking you to work. That's not—" Stopped. Started over. "I want you with me. Not to manage me or keep me from imploding. Just—as mine. As my person. That's it."

She held the silence this time, turning it over like a new soundboard. "I need to finish Cam's record. But I could fly out for weekends. Do a couple shows. New York for sure, because our parents are threatening to pull up on us if we don't visit soon. Once the EP wraps, I could join the last leg."

I blinked. "You'd do that?"

She gave me a crooked smile. "It'd be fun. I haven't been on tour since 2022. Kind of miss the adrenaline."

I tried to picture it: Shiloh, running my soundcheck without meaning to, then curled up in some weird hotel bed with me, arguing over how to optimize the setlist. And after, somewhere warm. Phones off. Just us, no label, no deadlines, no studio. Shiloh in the sun, doing absolutely nothing for once in her life. Me making her laugh about something stupid. No sound but the water and her voice. It was the first time in hours my chest didn't feel all tight.

"I don't want you to feel you have to," I said, softer.

She rolled her eyes. "You're such a dork. I want to see you perform. In person."

It got quiet again, but the good kind. The kind that feels like a deep breath before the first song of the night. She reached across the table, took my hand, her fingers warm against mine.

"But, E," she said, and now her voice went hard again. "You can't run."

I stared at her. "You're stuck with the lifetime warranty now, Shi. No refunds."

"You say that. But touring's chaos. I know what it does to you." She squeezed my fingers, not letting go. "If you get overwhelmed, you call me. You don't disappear. Not for a day. Not for an hour. Got it?"

My throat went tight. "Got it."

"You're going to be just fine." She stared me down as if she were etching it into my bones. Then her grip relaxed. "And if you're not, I'm here."

I was starting to believe her. For real this time. She kept me grounded in ways I was still figuring out how to admit. Not just my producer.

More than just someone I made music with. She was the reason I made it at all.

"I love you."

"I love you too, E." Her eyes got real soft, lashes long and pretty. I was getting used to seeing her look at me like that again.

"I gotta go," I said, halfway to whining. I'd rather spend the day snoring next to her instead. "Photoshoot. Then interview. Then some working lunch with the marketing team, and I already wish it was over."

Shiloh reached over to brush my lips with her thumb. I kissed her palm until she smiled.

"You'll survive."

"Barely." I stood up and started the daily hunt. I had exactly five minutes to get out. My keys were buried under one of Shiloh's records, which figures.

Jacket. Phone. Wallet. Again.

Shiloh watched from her chair, all folded up and judging. She wasn't wrong. "You're a mess."

"Your mess."

Shiloh snorted, like that was a win. She came over, and I didn't let her get another word in. I pulled her in close and kissed her fast, for real, none of that camera-ready stuff. She tasted like disaster coffee and something softer, something I didn't know the name for yet.

"I'll be back tonight," I said into her mouth. "Dinner. I'll grab Teriyaki."

"You better."

I kissed her again, slower. This one, I tried to keep. Then I was out the door, grabbing my bag, half-thinking about the schedule, half-thinking about Shiloh still standing there.

At the door, I glanced back. She was back at her desk already—glasses, headphones, morning light hitting her sideways. Barefoot, skin catching bronze in the sun. Looking like every reason I ever wrote a song.

And that was it. I knew I was coming back. Tonight. And tomorrow. And every night after.

Not because I was supposed to. Not because I was scared.

Just because this was it. This was home. *She* was home.

I closed the door behind me, already counting down the hours until I could come back.

Afterword

Here is where Bishop and Shiloh's story rests.

At this point in the story, Cam Wolfe and the unexplored conflict and tension between Romi Dulce really takes hold.

If you'd rather rest in Bishop and Shiloh's happy, settled vibes a little longer, here's a good place to rest until you are ready.

Cam and Romi's love story story awaits. The tone is harsher and the ground is more unforgiving, but it's the same world you've been reading about so far.

If you're curious about Cam's story, read on.

PREVIEW: Kissing The Opps

Cam

THERE'S ALWAYS THIS MOMENT when you step into a room and you know down in your bones that people were talking about you just seconds before.

You can smell it, the hot air left behind by a flash fire of gossip. I hit the afterparty alone, full face, custom button-down opened just low enough for the chain, but I didn't bother with my usual battery of handlers or hype people. Didn't need them. Tonight wasn't for peacocking; it was for watching.

Music: all bass, no mercy. The hotel suite was wall-to-wall with bodies—A&R babyfaces, local radio hosts, influencers filming everything, and at least one legit billionaire's son opening bottles nobody drank. The lights were so dim the only real glow came from phone screens and the DJ's booth.

People moved with the hyperfocus that comes after a big show, making sure they'd be seen in the right light, with the right drink, at the right distance from the main event. Me? I worked the outer edge, slow orbit, bouncing from cluster to cluster without ever getting pulled into anyone's gravity.

"—she straight up missed her mic cue—"

"—no, I saw the clip. It's already got four hundred thousand—"

Every snippet got sucked into the walls and twisted through the subs, but if you were listening for it, you could catch the important bits. I leaned against what was supposed to be marble but felt like fancy plastic, pretending to check my phone but really just watching the crowd move in tight, hungry loops.

You're never off, not for one second.

I did a quick scan to see if there was anyone I actually wanted to see. Stacks was probably still working the crowd outside; she played the long game with industry schmoozes. The only person who'd catch my eye tonight would be—*no*, not thinking about that yet.

What kept humming at the edge of every laugh, every gesture, was my name. Not shouted. Not even always spoken, but it was there, rippling through the room like a hidden track on a record you didn't ask for. Sometimes it was just the flick of an eyebrow or a micro-pause in someone's sentence, but you knew.

"That verse."

It didn't matter if they said it or just nodded toward the DJ. Every orbit in the room ran a gravity assist around those two words. Like the rest of the set had been prologue, and now nobody remembered who else even performed tonight.

I knew exactly which verse they meant. Romi's.

I'd watched it happen from backstage. When Romi hit the first line, the entire front row leaned in like they were about to catch something fragile. Then the second line—precision, no apology. It didn't burn; it froze.

And now, the room was full of it. People dissecting, recombining, searching for the next angle. The bloggers were already DMing their sources, making side bets about whether Romi would drop the track officially or just let the rumor mill do its job.

I sipped my orange drink, barely tasting it. Social media was going wild, I could tell by the constant glow from every wrist, every clutch bag. In an hour, there'd be a meme; by sunrise, there'd be a thinkpiece.

Not that I cared. Not that I'd ever show it.

Some girl in a corset and combat boots tried to sneak a photo of me from across the suite. I made eye contact, didn't blink, and she lost the nerve.

I let the conversations wrap around me like bad weather. People had opinions, but nobody wanted to say them straight to my face.

I found a dead spot near the bar and let the night glaze over me. There was a freedom in pretending not to care.

Someone touched my arm, a manicured finger light as a bug. Familiar dragon fruit body spray. I turned.

"Wow, so this is where the losers hang out," Skye said, nudging my foot with hers under the table. She dropped onto the ottoman across from me, legs crossed so high it should've been illegal, and grinned like she owned the copyright on mischief.

"You tracked me down just to call me a loser?" I didn't look up, just tapped a fingertip against my glass.

"Nah, just figured you'd appreciate the company." Her voice was the same as always. Like chewing Pop Rocks, all snap and sugar, but you might chip a tooth if you weren't careful. "You're taking it like a champ, though, gotta give you that. Most people would be hiding in the bathroom by now."

"I don't run from verses," I said, and she grinned, satisfied.

Every so often, I'd catch a stray word: "cam," "diss," "legend," "petty." My name and hers, flickering together.

She glanced around, making sure she had an audience, then leaned in, elbows on knees. "So, let's talk about that little show you put on tonight."

"Wasn't a little show," I said. "It was the whole headliner."

Skye smirked, fake-slow clap. "There she is. Miss Modesty." She tilted her head. "But let's be honest: you didn't expect that verse, did you?"

"I don't expect nothing from Romi except exactly what she did. Striking first when she feels cornered."

Skye laughed, a quick, rude bark that turned a couple of heads nearby. She tossed her hair and fished a gum pack out of her purse. "Oh my God, you are so full of shit. You live for this."

"Only when it's earned." I shrugged. "Tonight felt like someone swinging at shadows."

We let the moment hover. Skye wiggled her foot against my calf, absent-minded or not; I couldn't tell if it was a move or just her default setting. For a second, I almost forgot about the party, the whispers, the endless churn of opinion and ego.

"So, you and Romi," she said, quieter now, but with extra emphasis on the 'and' like it meant something. "That's a whole lot of yapping about each other for two people who allegedly can't stand each other."

"I don't hate her. But she definitely thinks I'm gunning for her spot, so..." I rolled my eyes. "Here we are."

Skye raised a brow. "Mm-hmm. This is me you're talking to, Cam, right?"

There was a pause, but it didn't get awkward. That was the weird thing about Skye: no matter how long you went without talking, she just slotted herself back into your life like a song you hadn't heard since high school but somehow still knew every lyric. We came up together. Same girl group, same dreams. Back when she was still Akasha, before the label decided "Skye Bella" would sell better.

Despite our history, I was grateful for her right now. Her chaos pulled me out of the spiral I'd been in since stepping off that stage. But I could already peep phones angled our way, catching glimpses of her foot still pressed against my leg, the easy way we fell back into each other's rhythm.

She switched topics without warning. "You know what's wild? I heard—like, from someone actually in the booth—that Romi wrote that verse ages ago. Sat on it for months, waiting for the right moment."

I set my glass down, slow. "You believe everything you hear in the booth?"

"Only the fun stuff." Skye's lips curled. "But you gotta admit, it's kinda hot."

Of course she sat on it. That verse had my name etched between the bars, even if she never said it. She'd been planning this. Thinking about it. Thinking about *me*.

I didn't give her the satisfaction, just shrugged. "Course she did. Can't let the new girls get too comfortable."

Skye looked me up and down, and for a second her expression got real. "You're taking this better than I thought," she said, almost admiring.

The only thing more predictable than a party winding down is the way it snaps back to life when the right person walks in.

Romi Dulce didn't just enter the suite—she commanded it, with a slowness that made sure every set of eyes got their fix before she even crossed the threshold. You could hear the ambient volume dip, just a notch, then surge back as everyone scrambled to look without looking.

All legs and curves in a cutout dress that looked like it came with its own insurance policy, smooth chocolate skin catching every light in the room like she was born to be photographed. Her hair fell in a perfect buss-down—not a strand out of place, which honestly should be illegal at this hour of the night.

She looked like she'd just stepped off a magazine cover that I'd never be cool enough to grace. The thought didn't sting. Much.

Those blackout-dark sunglasses didn't come off, not even indoors. Of course they didn't. Pure Romi: never let anyone catch you looking back, not even once. She kept her face blank, lips done up so dark they almost disappeared into the glare. Like she'd made out with midnight and left some of it on her mouth, just to prove she could.

I watched a few people stiffen their backs, suddenly remember they had somewhere else to be. The DJ, sensing the shift, faded out the trap and swapped in a low-key classic, as if he was paying respect.

I didn't expect her to acknowledge me.

But she did. Just a turn in my direction, sunglasses never moving, but her chin lifted with that particular brand of arrogance I knew by heart. A smirk ghosted across those dark lips—barely there, but unmistakable. Like she'd spotted something amusing and wanted me to know she'd seen it. The message was crystal clear even through tinted lenses. I see you sitting there, and I'm not impressed.

I met her energy with an eyebrow raise. Not shrinking.

The moment lasted less than a heartbeat, but it dropped the temperature in the room by a solid ten degrees. Romi turned away, gliding toward the balcony where three execs were already fighting for her time. Someone passed her a drink, and she accepted it without a word, never breaking stride.

My pulse tripped, then settled, like a runner catching their second wind.

Skye leaned in. "If you're not gonna start drama, maybe you should at least start something else."

"Like what?"

She shrugged, eyes wide. "A fight. A rumor. A bar. People are hungry."

I almost laughed. Instead, I let the words tumble around my head, stacking themselves into rhythm, then rhyme. The first bar was easy: *Queen in leather, stiff walk, ice grip, She freeze every room just to feel like she it—*

I didn't need to write it down. It lived in my chest, hot and restless.

Tomorrow, there'd be messages blowing up my phone. Some blogger would probably turn tonight into a whole thinkpiece. And yeah, there'd be another verse eventually. Mine this time.

But for now, I had bars cooking in my chest.

Also By L.M. Bennett

Other Series

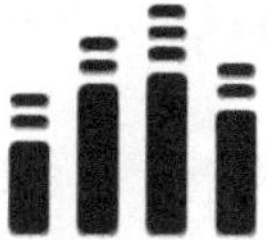

Competing Desires is the Las Vegas-based trilogy of love and rivalry in the worlds of Championship Poker, Mixed Martial Arts and Racing. High angst, action-packed, firecracker slow burn sports romances. Titles in the series include:

Bad Beat

Pit Stop

Tap Out

Love Cynics Anonymous is a series of loosely-interconnected stories about young women who are avoiding love, but find it anyway. Some even manage not to mess it up. Sweet and spicy, slow burn romances. Other titles in the series include:

Corked!: An Enemies-to-Lovers Short (no spice)

Lesbian Speed Dating: A Short Story (no spice)

(re)twist – A [Hendrix/Fatima] Short Story

Bespoke: A Novella

String Theory: A Valentine's Day Novelette (no spice)

Crushed: A Novelette

You Were Almost Home

Hot Mic is an upcoming series about love, hip hop and authenticity set in Los Angeles. Titles in the series include:

The Art of Going Rogue

Track Four Is Not About You

Kissing The Opps (Serial)

Christmas Curveballs is what it looks when it's Christmas and you're totally over it, but you meet your person because the universe has jokes. Titles in the series include:

The Cynic's Christmas Conundrum

The Connoisseur's Christmas Courtship (McKenna's Story)

The Chef's Christmas Charade